NYE, R.

THE MEMOIRS OF
LORD BYRON
A NOVEL

Also by Robert Nye

POETRY

Juvenilia 1, *Scorpion Press*, 1961
Juvenilia 2, *Scorpion Press*, 1963
Darker Ends, *Calder & Boyars*, 1969
Divisions on a Ground, *Carcanet Press*, 1976
A Collection of Poems 1955–1988, *Hamish Hamilton*, 1989

FICTION

Doubtfire, *Calder & Boyars*, 1967
Tales I Told My Mother, *Calder & Boyars*, 1969
The Same Old Story, *Penguin Modern Stories 6*, 1970
Falstaff, *Hamish Hamilton*, 1976
Merlin, *Hamish Hamilton*, 1978
Faust, *Hamish Hamilton*, 1980
The Voyage of the Destiny, *Hamish Hamilton*, 1982
The Facts of Life and other fictions, *Hamish Hamilton*, 1983

FOR CHILDREN

The Bird of the Golden Land, *Hamish Hamilton*, 1980
Harry Pay the Pirate, *Hamish Hamilton*, 1981
Three Tales, *Hamish Hamilton*, 1983

EDITIONS

A Choice of Sir Walter Ralegh's Verse, *Faber*, 1972
William Barnes, Selected Poems, *Carcanet Press*, 1973
A Choice of Swinburne's Verse, *Faber*, 1973
The Faber Book of Sonnets, *Faber*, 1976
The English Sermon 1750–1850, *Carcanet Press*, 1976

THE MEMOIRS OF

LORD BYRON

A NOVEL

BY

ROBERT NYE

HAMISH HAMILTON

LONDON

HAMISH HAMILTON LTD

Published by the Penguin Group
27 Wrights Lane, London W8 5TZ, England
Viking Penguin Inc, 40 West 23rd Street, New York, New York 10010, U.S.A.
Penguin Books Australia Ltd, Ringwood, Victoria, Australia
Penguin Books Canada Ltd, 2801 John Street, Markham, Ontario, Canada L3R 1B4
Penguin Books (N.Z.) Ltd, 182–190 Wairau Road, Auckland 10, New Zealand

Penguin Books Ltd, Registered Offices: Harmondsworth, Middlesex, England

First published in Great Britain 1989 by
Hamish Hamilton Ltd

1 3 5 7 9 10 8 6 4 2

British Library Cataloguing in Publication Data
A CIP data for this book is available from the British Library

ISBN 0-241-12873-0

Printed in Great Britain by
Butler and Tanner Ltd, Frome, Somerset

CONTENTS

Contents (*continued*)

I would to Heaven that I were so much clay,
As I am blood, bone, marrow, passion, feeling –
Because at least the past were passed away,
And for the future – (but I write this reeling,
Having got drunk exceedingly to-day,
So that I seem to stand upon the ceiling)
I say – the future is a serious matter –
And so – for God's sake – hock and soda-water!

CHAPTER ONE

I Lose Some of my Virginity

My passions were developed very early – so early, that few will believe me, now I am to state the period, and the facts which accompanied it. Still, I, George Gordon, sixth Lord Byron, am a plain man, and my way is to begin with the beginning, so here goes.

My father died when I was three years old, naming me in his will as sole heir to his real and personal estate. He had raked and run his way through my mother's small fortune at the time, and that of another little heiress wife before her, so all that I inherited were the debts and the funeral expenses. I do not think my father loved my mother beyond reason, since at the time of his death he had absented himself from his creditors to France, where his sister had a house at Valenciennes, while his wife and his only son lived a pinched life in furnished lodgings in Aberdeen. I heard from my aunt once that my father said of my mother that she was very amiable at a distance, but he defied all the apostles to live with her two months. From the same aunt, I heard that the only thing she remembered him saying about me was that it was impossible I should ever walk, as I was club-footed. In this, my father was right about my mother, but wrong about me. It is true that I have a *cloven hoof* – that is to say a small deformity of the right foot, the toes of which are turned or bent inwards, a consequence I believe of my mother's behaviour when she was introducing me to the world, since her prudery made her reject the necessary medical attendance. It is also true that all my life I have had to wear a special shoe because of this, the iron braces and the hot wax having failed. But I ran before I could walk, and I now limp faster than most. Am I not *Le Diable Boiteux* – no angel who has tripped his foot against a star, but without doubt the very Devil incarnate? All the same, it is tedious to go through life walking on the outside of one foot, and in my next existence I expect to have two if not four legs by way of compensation. Alternatively, if Christianity has it right, and our carcasses are to rise again, then I trust that I shall have two decent feet when the trumpet sounds, or I shall be sadly behind in the squeeze into Paradise. What comfort to be a cripple, nevertheless. When one limb is weak another invariably makes up for it. As the queen of the Amazons said: '*The lame fuck best.*' (I am also rather good at standing still.)

I was not so young when my father died but that I perfectly remember him, and had very early a horror of matrimony from the sight of domestic broils. All the same, I have to admit that my mother, once out of her wedded bliss and with no prospect of its return, seemed to miss something. My father's death left the sad creature inconsolable. Having wept and wailed her way up and down most of the streets of granite Aberdeen, this wild provincial widow turned her love and her hate headlong on me. She was not a bad woman, my prodigal father's relict, but she was not a good mother. In fact,

I Lose Some of my Virginity

I think it is not too much, now that she's dead, to admit that my mother was almost certainly mad – to say she was in her senses, would be condemning her as a criminal. (She died, be it noted, this lineal if zigzag descendant of King James I, of a fit of apoplexy brought on by reading an upholsterer's bill.) All my happy cat-and-mouse childhood days she kissed me and cuffed me by turns. Sometimes she'd say I was just as wicked as my father. Sometimes she'd spoil me with a foolish fondness. I didn't know which was the worse, and I don't know now. She gave me being, of course, but I never asked for that, and besides all the best philosophers agree that not to have been born is better. In her person, my mother was small and plump, with a long nose that turned up at everything, and too high a colour by half. She possessed this quite endearing talent for dressing in a style that combined the shabby with the tawdry. Loving or hating, in or out of her corsets, she lived her whole life in hurricane bursts, so far as I could see. Often, when she was in full blast, I wished I could be swallowed up by an earthquake, provided my eloquent mother was not in it. She attacked me with pokers and tongs, and, when that failed, caresses. Her most memorable maternal endearments were to call me her '*lame brat*' or her '*Caliban*'. Peace be with her! I will mention just one incident as proof of our unique affection for each other. One evening, when in a fit of frenzy she had raked up the ashes of my father, abused him, and said (making a death-rattle of the rolled 'r') that I too would turn out to be a true *Byrrone*, which was always the worst epithet she was able to invent, I observed her looking at me so sensitively over a venison pie that later I crept out of the house and hurried to the apothecary's, demanding to know if my mother had been there to purchase poison. 'No,' said the apothecary, smiling. 'So why do you smile then?' I asked him. 'Because,' said the apothecary, 'Mrs Byron called in here just ten minutes ago to ask the same question about you.'

When I was nine years old, this meek mamma of mine put me in the hands of a young Scotch governess, a devout Calvinist by the name of May Gray. (Never trust a woman whose name rhymes with itself.) This governess took me to spend the summer with her in the valley of the Dee, at a farmhouse not far from Abergeldie. It was the first time I ever saw our northern Alps, and I was soon an enthusiast of crags and cataracts, especially the eagle peak of Loch-na-garr, whose summit, the seat of eternal snows, came sometimes into view above the clouds. I walked with difficulty, but wandered at will, soothed and inspired by the grandeur of the scenery. I exercised my body and gratified my spirit by teetering on the brinks of precipices, delighting in joining the wail of my nature to the voice of the universe. To Miss Gray I owe my love of mountains, my knowledge of the Scriptures, and my inoculation with too much Calvinism for either faith or unfaith in Christianity. To Miss Gray, also, I owe the precocious development of my sexual passions. It was this peculiar young woman's pleasure to read to me from the Bible in the mornings, to beat me in the afternoons until my flesh throbbed and my small bones ached, and then to come naked into my bed at night to play tricks with my person. No doubt at first she only meant to clasp my penis with a pure Platonic squeeze, but it soon grew otherwise. Besides, even at nine I was no kind of Platonist myself. In her person, Miss Gray was white, and tall, and thin. (I hate a dumpy woman.) She was also charming, chaste, and twenty-three. When I say charming I mean that she had cool fingers. When I say chaste I mean that *I* was never permitted to touch *her*. Poor little fellow! In feelings I was quick as Ovid's Miss Medea. As for Miss Gray, she sang to herself as she played, or whispered Scotch encouragements in my ear. I cannot remember the songs. The encouragements I could not understand, and did not need. Truth to tell, I found my governess's games in my bed not unpleasant and I said nothing about them to my mother at the time. It is plain to me now that I owe this rampant religious succubus a very great deal, and not all of it bad. Her erotic dominion over me lasted about two years. As to the Bible readings, I disliked the New Testament but quite enjoyed the Old, especially the 93rd Psalm and the tale of Cain and Abel. When I considered that I had learned sufficient at Miss Gray's wise hands, I took an opportunity to mention her extracurricular lessons to our family lawyer, John Hanson. He told my mother the dowager. The predestinated milkmaid was sent packing.

Perhaps this is one of the reasons which caused the anticipated melancholy of my thoughts – having anticipated life. My earliest poems, after all, are the thoughts of one at least ten years older than the age at which they were written: I don't mean for their solidity, but their experience. The first two cantos of *Childe Harold* were completed when I was twenty-two, and they are written as if by a man older than I shall probably ever be.

I begin these *Memoirs* half-way through my thirtieth year to hell, here at my best stopping-place so far, the Palazzo Mocenigo, in Venice, on Friday the thirteenth of July, 1818, recovering from a dose of the clap and having nothing worse to do. As to why I write at all – it was once because my mind and heart were full of stuff which needed out, but now it is merely to avoid idleness, though idleness in a hot country can be a pleasure.

CHAPTER TWO

I Lose Some More of my Virginity

I HAVE JUST BEEN observing from my balcony a little adventure amid the comings and goings on the Grand Canal. There was one gondola with a young man lying in it, wearing a yellow cloak and trailing his hand in the slimy green water. He lay there for an hour, with no gondolier to guide him, basking in the morning sun like a sick lizard. Above, on the bridge, a dozen children were snarling and spitting and throwing shells and oranges at each other in some minor internecine conflict. Then one of the children tumbled headlong into the water. None of his enemies or companions took the slightest notice. Nor did the young man in the yellow cloak. But my bastard infant daughter Allegra, watching from another window of the palazzo, saw the boy threshing about and began to scream, supposing that he would surely drown, though most of these urchins are absolute water-rats and quite as much at home in the water as on the bridges and in the alleys. Allegra's screams woke the excitement of all my dogs and birds and monkeys and in a minute the whole house was an uproar of noise, the very windows throbbing and shaking with the row, and Margarita's shrill voice soaring over all, until my gondolier went down the steps to fish the wretched child out with a hook. Allegra wanted me to keep him for her, but I said that his mother might miss him. The boy ran off cursing – crossing himself with one hand while he clutched his balls for luck with the other, sure that the English milord was the Devil. (*Mem*: I must explain Margarita's position in my household before the end of this chapter, but this morning I am still getting used to it myself.) Through all this adventure the young man in the yellow cloak took not a whit of notice. When I shut Allegra up again with her nurse, and took these sheets of paper upon the balcony to resume the writing of my story out-of-doors, the lizard was still lying there on his back in his blue-painted gondola, now with his face half-buried in a melon. Such is Venice. I like this place. It suits me.

I could never say half as much for Aberdeen. When I was five years old, my mother sent me to a day school kept by a Mr Bowers in that harsh city. The charge was a mere five shillings a quarter. Mr Bowers' standard of teaching being about commensurate with his fees, during the time I spent there I learned little except to repeat by rote the first lesson in a book of words of one syllable: *God made man – let us love Him*. When proof was required at home that I could read, I repeated these words with the most rapid fluency, but when my mother tired of this parrot performance and turned over the page for me I continued to repeat them, so that the narrow boundaries of my accomplishment were detected and my ears boxed (which they did not deserve, seeing that it was by *ear* only that I had acquired my letters). Mr Bowers, as I recall, was known as '*Bodsy* Bowers' by reason of his dapperness. His favourite form of exercise consisted in rubbing his cocker against the napes of the necks of his pupils, as he bent over us where we sat obedient at our desks. This was performed through his nankeen breeches, so no one could ever exactly be sure what to complain of. Returning to his care, I learned soon enough that the second page of my primer actually contained the words, *God made Satan – and Satan made sin.* I considered this very true, and I still do. At that school I was known as Mrs Byron's crooked devil, mostly on account of my foot.

There followed a short series of private tutors, all of whom had a lively time of it with my mother, yet who still managed between them to do a certain amount of damage on me. The first of these was a very pious, clever little clergyman named Ross, under whom I began to take a keen interest in history, a subject which became something of a passion, especially when we got to lists of ships and captains and kings reigning. I remember this Reverend Mr Ross also introduced my mother to the severe delights of a certain church in Aberdeen where the preaching was even more full of hell-fire than is the wont. She dragged me along to listen and be frightened in her wake, until the Sunday came when sitting beside her on the pew I contrived to abstract the hat-pin from her hat and stick it into her fat arm at a crucial point in the sermon, so that her shriek provided a suitable exclamation mark to the preacher's promises of the fate awaiting the damned. My next tutor was called Paterson, another Presbyterian, a deadly serious, saturnine, but kind young man, with a boil behind his left ear and a penchant for sniffing my mother's footwear which I discovered by accident one afternoon when I opened the broom cupboard door and found him busy with his tool in one hand and his nose in a riding boot. Of course I seized a tin of blacking and pretended I had noticed nothing. He was the son of a shoemaker, and picked his melancholy nose as well as his boil, but he was a good scholar as well as a foot-fetichist as is common with the Scotch. With Paterson I began Latin, and Roman history, which I adored, especially the filthy loves of gods and goddesses, and continued till I went to the Aberdeen Grammar School, which had a roof thatched with heather and a grate where we burned peat in winter to keep warm. Under that roof I threaded all the classes to the fourth, when I was recalled to England (where I had been hatched) by the demise of my great-uncle, the 5th Lord Byron. This critical event occurred when I was ten years old.

On the whole, I cannot help thinking that it was a misfortune in disguise that I ever succeeded to the family title. I was not in the direct line of succession, as I shall explain. Being too much impressed by the adventitious splendour suddenly bestowed upon me has done its bit to warp and spoil my character. Even as infant heir I was perhaps over-conscious of the added importance. A lady, a friend of my mother's, thinking to compliment me, once remarked over her currant scone, 'We shall some day have the pleasure of reading your speeches in the House of Commons, Geordie.' 'Indeed, I hope not,' I replied. 'If you read any speech of mine, it will have been made in the House of Lords.' I was nine when I said that, having fallen heir to my great-uncle William, the fifth and wicked Lord, in 1794, at the age of six, when his son my cousin was killed in Corsica, at the siege of Calvi, where Nelson lost an eye.

Now the long-anticipated wonder had come to pass. I was, as my mother said in her Hyperborean accents, '*a lor' a' lang laist*'. There is no doubt that it was a supreme thrill for her, after her years of civil war with the butchers and bakers and candlestick-makers of Aberdeen. I remember that she pointed out to me that one of the noblest privileges of being a *lor'* was that *lors* could not be imprisoned for debt. As for myself, the great transformation came, I must confess, as something of a disappointment. I had expected it to improve my soul, and it did nothing even for my digestive tract. I remember, when I was told the news, running up to a mirror and asking my mother if she could see any difference in me now that I had become *Lord* Byron, for I could see none myself. At school the next morning, when my name was first called with the glorious addition of '*Dominus*', I could not find voice for the customary '*Adsum*', and after a short embarrassed interval of silence, I burst into tears. These things are pardonable in a child, but there are less pardonable things in my life since which make me think that I might have had a better chance to be a gentleman if I had never been a lord. Egotism combines too readily with the fact of rank. My aristocracy is very fierce.

My next school, to which I was dispatched as a boarder between the ages of ten and thirteen, was Dr Glennie's, at Dulwich. Here my mamma continued her unfortunate interest in my education by constantly taking me away, sometimes for weeks on end, furiously resenting the natural expostulations and protests of the master. I have never forgotten the moment when I stood at a gabled window with one of my classmates at Dulwich as we both watched a familiar female figure huffing and puffing up the steps of the academy, waving her arms in the air, shouting for me and munching raspberries, and my companion turned to me and coolly said, 'Byron, your mother is a fool.' It was a discovery I had already made for myself. 'I know it,' I replied. At last, in April, 1801, at the age of thirteen and a squeak, I proceeded to Harrow, my mother having been granted £300 from the Civil List to provide for my education.

I hated Harrow for the first three years or so, and not just because most of the other fellows were richer and some of the bigger ones at different times liked to torment me by putting my warped foot into a bucket of hot water, by holding me over candleflames in the dormitory to toast my arse, and by smearing my pintle with boot polish and tickling it with peacock feathers after Lights Out. My instruction by May Gray in the facts of life had been very sound so far as it went. But I now learned that there were other tricks and other vices, none of them greatly to my taste, truth to tell, though I had of course the natural curiosity of the schoolboy and never ceased to wonder at the way my tool responded almost against my will when older fellows snatched my breeches down, and grabbed at me, or when I was beaten on the buttocks with the cane by tutors or prefects for some real or invented transgression meriting such chastisement. However, I never went the whole hog with any of the boys at Harrow, young or old, and the story of my first complete sexual experience with one of my own gender must await another chapter. May Gray and such matters aside, I must admit that I

F/348859

arrived at Harrow ill-prepared for the shocks of life, and with the marks of my previous provincial status patent all over me. Though I had accumulated a fair fleece of general knowledge from wide but unsystematic combing through books, I was woefully backward in the class-room arts and graces now required, and morbidly sensitive besides at the thought of being placed with boys younger than myself. In general I should say that any life in common with others could never be congenial to one of my temperament which – like the peak of a lofty mountain, or a ripe fart in a colander – seeks for solitude. The discipline of the college suited still less my native freedom of character. Its pleasures were to me annoy-ances, its tastes and habits quite repulsive. At least in the event I was spared the indignity of being placed with boys younger than myself, by the consideration of my headmaster, Dr Drury, who promised that for the present I should not be placed at all, so that I might have the chance of equipping myself decently. This amiable doctor was one of the few people having to do with me in my early years who took any pains to understand my curious and wayward temperament and treat me with respect. It is a pleasure to remember that he disciplined me only with a silken string, my old preceptor. I look on him still as a father, whose warnings I have remembered but too well, though too late, when I have erred, and whose counsel I have but followed when I have done well or wisely. He had a great notion, Dr Drury, that I should turn out to be an orator. My first Harrow verses, a translation of a chorus from the *Prometheus* of Aeschylus, were received by him with a proper lack of enthusiasm. No one had the least notion

in those days that I should subside my soul and other parts into poesy.

My friendships at Harrow were matters of the utmost intensity, though like most other ardent youthful attachments their fervour was apt to exceed their durability. In short, they were no doubt too romantic to last. My school friendships were to me passions (for I was always violent), but I do not think that there is any which has endured till now (to be sure, some have been cut short by death). Hunter, Harness, Curzon, Long and Tatersall were my principal friends; Clare, Dorset, Charles Gordon, De Bath, Claridge with his pock-marked face and John Wingfield were my juniors and favourites, whom I spoilt by indulgence. I never abused any of my fags, when it was my turn to hold the reins of power and wield the whip. This, I may claim, was a little unusual in a time and place where every boy of good looks (even 'Dorothy' Claridge) had a female nickname, and a boy who yielded his person to an older lover was known simply as the elder lad's 'bitch'. The talk in the dormitories at Harrow was of the grossest character in my day (it may be different now, although I doubt it), and there were repulsive scenes of onanism, mutual masturbation, and obscene orgies of naked boys in bed together. I held apart from all this not from prudishness but by reason of a natural fleshly repugnance. I have never much relished or enjoyed the physical society of my own sex. Yet, to a youth such as I was, abounding with the most passionate feelings, and finding sympathy with only the ruder parts of my nature at home, the little world of school afforded a vent for the affections, and was sure to call them forth in their

most ardent form. Accordingly, the friendships which I contracted both at school and college were, as I say, little less than passions.

My dearest friend at Harrow was without doubt John Fitzgibbon, the 2nd Earl of Clare. His father had been the Lord Chancellor of Ireland, but Clare himself succeeded to the family title the year before he came to school. He was eleven; I was then fifteen. Clare! Friend of my youth! I never hear the name 'Clare' without a beating of the heart even now, and I write it down here with the feelings of 1803–4–5 intact *ad infinitum.* (Not even the woman whose real name is Jane Clairmont could spoil the sound of the word for me by changing *her* first name to 'Claire'.) My friend Clare, unlike La Clairmont, had no guile in him. On the contrary, there was a sort of illumination about this young fellow, a translucent quality. I recall the first time that I saw him, in a classroom, sitting in profile two desks away, writing about Byzantium and looking half like an angel and half as though he had been sculptured out of pale butter. With a face and airs like that, of course, he was much pursued by the grosser pupils. So I became his hero and his champion, protecting him from bullies and buggers alike. We swam together: that was our only real physical contact, when sometimes our bodies would brush against each other in the water. Otherwise – and I may state plainly that I do not regret this – I never laid a finger on Clare, nor he on me. Our friendship was a pure thing right through school, and therefore all the more precious to both of us. I recall without embarrassment that we talked a lot, as solemn lads do, about love and death and God and the meaning of life.

He said to me once, as we sat in the chapel: 'Byron, you are a poet.' This observation arrested me. I had by then already written verses, for reasons I shall disclose in due course; but there was no way that my friend Clare could have known of these, and certainly I did not yet think of myself as *being* a poet at all, let alone go about proclaiming the condition. 'Why do you say so?' I asked him. He laughed. 'Because you've been talking to me for half an hour about truth,' he said, 'and I haven't been able to understand a word of it!' It is not too much to say that in that moment, sitting in a mote-filled shaft of sunlight beside my friend, I learned three things – one thing about him, and two about myself. Concerning Clare, I saw that beauty did not preclude banality or ignorance. Concerning myself, I saw first that my realising as much about Clare did not prevent me loving him still as my friend, and second that I wanted above all his original statement ('*Byron, you are a poet*') to be true. In that instant, Clare became my brother. Without knowing the importance of what he said – intending it, for all I know, quite trivially – nevertheless something in him had *recognised* something in me. I could have kissed him; but of course I didn't. Later, I wrote some lines of verse about him, in imitation of Valerius Flaccus, sweet yet artful, already lamenting lost youth before I had lost it. Clare handed them back to me, smiling, but offered no comment. Some years later, on the day before I first set out for Greece, I solicited his company only for the Earl to prefer to go shopping with his mother and his sisters. But I count that a minor blemish on a beautiful friendship, and I trust that I will not now be misunderstood either by my contemporaries or any scandal-minded posterity if I roundly declare that I love Clare better than any male thing in the world, while in the same breath conceding that there may be some distance-bred sentimentality and much nostalgia for the idealism of my schooldays in this love.

If I had my full share of school friendships, loving with exceeding tenderness my friends from Claridge up to Clare, so I had also my full share of school fights, hating the ranks of my enemies too with all the fury that comes from passion. 'Milling' holds a recognised position at Harrow, where the tradition has always been to let it take its course unless the odds are manifestly unfair, a wise provision probably which on the whole makes for peace by allowing little natural outbursts of violence. I had no less than seven fights in all, of which I won five, drew one, and lost one. In the last case everyone was against me, and I was not even allowed a second. My lameness was of course unfavourable to me in this rough form of exercise, especially if my adversary could manage to keep me out until I grew tired. However, I can say that this was not easily done. I was always more ready to give a blow than to take one. A lame man has a horse's kick in his arms, and I often succeeded in making short work of my opponents.

My school career, then, was stormy as well as romantic. I was never a popular boy, any more than I have ever been a popular man, though at Harrow I *led* latterly. It was only 'latterly', too, in my last year and a half there, that the love of school, which, against all the odds, is so peculiarly strong in most Harrow boys for the rest of their lives, took root and remained in my heart. (I wrote '*rot*' there, in that last sentence, and mean both, though I've corrected myself.) As for this general theme of turbulence – I always have loved a row, I freely admit it. With Henry Drury, the head-master's son, in whose house finally I was placed, I got on terribly, so much so that the admirable and amiable Dr D was almost driven to insist upon my leaving before my time. Out of school my chief delight was in swimming and cricket. I even earned a place in the Harrow team that played Eton in the year of Trafalgar, but was dismissed for eleven in the first innings and seven in the second, and had to have another boy to run for me, on account of my foot. It amused me, though, that I did better than the player immediately above me in the batting order, since his name was Shakespeare.

My happiest hours at Harrow, when all is said and done, were spent in my own company, at a particular place in the churchyard adjacent to the school, near the footpath, on the brow of the hilly part which looks towards London, where there is a smooth flat grey tomb under a large tree, an elm. I used to like to lie on this tomb's top. I would lie there for hours and hours, sometimes devouring for my own pleasure books of travels and shipwrecks, but more often thinking of nothing in particular, until the stone grew warm against my back. I cannot now remember the name of the person buried there. Peachie, was it, or Peachey?

My home here on the Grand Canal has a new mistress. I saw her first when riding along the Brenta – a Venetian girl with large black eyes (I'm very fond of handsome eyes), a face like Faustina's, and the figure of Juno, tall and energetic as a pythoness, with dark hair streaming in the moonlight. I asked her name, proposed a rendezvous. She told me she is called Margarita Cogni and announced almost in the same breath that she was quite prepared to be my mistress as she is married and all the married women in Venice take lovers if they can. 'Why's that?' I demanded, intending to tease her. By way of answer, my glorious Zenobia just raised her right hand and chafed the thumb of it with the index finger. 'My darling girl,' I protested, 'you are too beautiful to require charity.' At that, she laughed, revealing a most splendid set of teeth, and placed her hands on her hips. 'Milord thinks so?' she said. 'Well, if you saw my hut and my food, you would not make that little mistake.' We made love first on the floor of a ruined chapel. I remember the place smelled of mould and her cunt tasted of anchovies. Of all the women I have known, I consider this Margarita the most Gargantuan in her sexual appetite. The second time I keyed her, under the stars to the howling of wild dogs, she took trouble to warn me that her husband is a baker by vocation, and very fierce. I can believe he'd need to be, to please her. Margarita is twenty-two, and can neither read nor write, one of those women who may be made anything. I am sure that if I put a poniard in the hand of this one, she would plunge it wherever I told her – and into *me*, if I offended her. Nipples so sharp when roused that you could cut your lips upon them; thighs like a triumphal arch; long, well-muscled legs; and a mouth like a red Hell. I like this kind of animal, and am quite sure that I should have preferred Medea to any other woman that ever breathed. At all events, last night on stepping from my gondola I found this magnificent creature waiting for me on the steps of the palazzo. I gave her cakes and claret, and she sucked me off. I ate a strawberry biscuit; then I fucked her. This morning she refuses to go back to her husband, the terrible baker; says, indeed, that he's '*un becco etico*' (a consumptive cuckold) compared with her new lord and master.

CHAPTER THREE

I Inherit a Great Number of Tree Stumps

Here I sit by the light of my candles and watch the summer rain run down the pane. It is an hour and a half before midnight. Out there, the pimps will be making their little coloured lanterns wink and dance in the doorways of the whorehouses on the other side of the Rialto, and the gondolas will be depositing more fashionable and expensive ladies for the usual party at the Countess Benzoni's or the usual ball at the Countess Albrizzi's. This is my fair foul spiritual home, but tonight I choose to sit at my desk apart from it, making black marks on a white sheet of paper. And instead of the open-armed, sweet-scented, *matto grosso* Paradise which is Venice, I must write of that tight-buttocked bloody island where I was born....

Having, for the sake of convenience if not coherence, placed together in one chapter my more or less fond recollections of my schooldays, I shall now cast back a few strokes in the story and take myself up again at the point already mentioned where, in my eleventh year of blessed mortal damnation, I was brought down from North Britain to enter upon my estates as the sixth Lord Byron. Picture the scene, dear reader, as an agreeably excited little party drives up within sight of the domains of Newstead Abbey, in the shire of Nottingham, family seat of the Byrons, on the edge of Sherwood Forest, one bright blustery morning in the autumn of 1798. With me in the chaise are my mother in a purple hat and the succubus May Gray clutching a Bible in her paw to ward off the evil English. Mamma, unable as always to resist an opportunity for drama, enquires of the bearded ruffian at the Newstead toll-bar, 'And wha's estate may this be?' 'It was Lord Byron's, madam,' says the man. 'But he is lately dead.' 'Ah see,' declares my mother. 'And wha' maight be the heir o' thon Lorrd Byrrone?' (Stroking her hat, rolling her eyes, and smiling fit to bust.) 'Well, madam,' says the worthy troll politely, 'they do say 'tis a little lad what lives in Aberdeen.' Whereupon – peals of 'girlish' laughter from my proud sly maternal parent as '*And here he is, God bless him!*' cries May Gray, kissing me wetly and noisily on the nose, bringing the farce to a satisfactory climax as usual. Well, I can remember this now without too much shame, vomit, or squirming. It was, you might notice, one of the few happy and innocent moments in the life of the three of us.

Alas and wheesht (as my mother would have said), but it turned out to be a lie, that happy moment, as we learned all too soon. My inheriting the title brought hardly a penny of immediate money with it, the estate being mortgaged and encumbered up to the chimney-tops. In the misanthropic butcher hands of my late great-uncle William, Newstead (originally a religious house built by King Henry II in his guilt after the murder of Thomas à Becket) had suffered as grievously as at any time in its long history. I think it not too much to say that everything was in ruin, from the bedrooms down to the beer cellars. Looking upon my ancestral house for the first time, I felt my hair twine like a knot of snakes upon my head. The dirt and the disorder were formidable beyond belief, with the attics full of bats and empty bottles, and docks and thistles and deadly nightshade growing through the floorboards in the larder. All the same, I suppose that the estate itself would have offered about three thousand acres of prime parkland had my great-uncle not seen fit to slaughter all of its trees to spite his relatives. I may say that I do not believe my great-uncle William to have been a pure-minded or fanatically dedicated tree-murderer. He cut down some of the trees to pay his debts. Unfortunately he ran out of trees somewhat before he ran out of debts, and so I inherited not three thousand acres of prime parkland but three thousand acres of rotting tree stumps. One way and another, my great-uncle William assuredly must have hated trees, particularly elms and oaks. I can understand his passion, though I do not share it. (*Daffodils* are more in my line of abhorrence, on account of Wordsworth.) As for the Abbey, there was a hole in its roof big enough to drop a horse through, its walls were covered with mushrooms, and the grand hall was ankle-deep in dead leaves. All that remained of the chapel itself was a skeleton of stones shrouded in cobwebs and crowned with rusty ivy. The whole place smelled deliciously of earthworms.

I regret now that I never met my great-uncle William, the fifth Lord Byron. He must have been a villain after my own heart. I collected many anecdotes about him. He always went armed, a pistol in each pocket, and dined at night with these flintlocks set out neat beside his cutlery. He built two small forts on the shore of the lake in front of the Abbey and there superintended somewhat in the manner of Tristram Shandy's even greater uncle Toby with his soldiers, complicated naval manoeuvres and engagements in miniature, firing at dozens of model ships with a brace of toy cannon. Other stories I heard about him may have been coloured in the passage of the years, but they do at least indicate some of the rich black splendour of his character. (Man's a strange animal, and of all mankind great-uncles are the strangest.) He is said to have shot his coachman dead on the spot for some trivial disregard of orders (turning left instead of turning right) and then bundled the fellow's corpse into the coach where his wife was sitting nagging, and, mounting the box, driven the grisly couple home himself. The beauty of this is that it was the wife who had complained at the turning left. It would appear, however, that as a cure for nagging, compelling the nagger to keep company in a coach with the corpse of a sinister coachman simply doesn't work, since later my great-uncle William is reported to have attempted to murder the same wife by hurling her into the Newstead pond. Small wonder, you might think, that the poor talkative lady found herself obliged to pack her bags and leave him. (Married Byrons very rarely live together until death do them part.) Still and all, I do not myself believe that my great-uncle William ever tried to hurl his wife into the Newstead pond. The Newstead pond is only three feet deep, and no good for the murder of even a very small wife.

By his last decade my great-uncle William had

developed all the attributes of a positive recluse. Some say that this withdrawal from the world was not monastic, but came as a result of a duel which he fought with his neighbour Mr William ('Stinker') Chaworth, of Annesley Hall. The quarrel arose from the two gentlemen holding different opinions on the important philosophical subject of the best method of preserving game; they fell into a fierce and abstruse argument about this at the Notts Club Dinner, held at the Star and Garter Tavern, in Pall Mall. It was Mr Chaworth, a regular bully and braggart, who seems to have been chiefly to blame for the debate turning into a duel. They fought in a locked room by the light of a single tallow candle, with no seconds or other witnesses. Mr Chaworth made a pass which in the gloom he probably believed to have been effectual, but his sword had only become entangled in my great-uncle William's fancy waistcoat, and while he was leaning over gloating and enquiring as to the extent of the presumed damage my great-uncle finished him off quick with a single thrust in the belly. For this my great-uncle was sent to the Tower and tried for murder in Westminster Hall by his peers of the House of Lords, but he was convicted only of manslaughter, and escaped further punishment on paying his fees. I do not myself credit the sentimental notion that my great-uncle turned his back on the world because he was eaten up by remorse. I think he was a man who liked shutting his front door, that's all. If he had felt so unconscionably guilty would he have kept the sword with which he spitted Mr Chaworth hanging from a meat-hook on his bedroom wall? It was there when he died. I inherited it.

Anyway, for whatever reason, or none, my great-uncle William spent the remainder of his life, after the duel, cutting down trees and living in his dilapidated Abbey with only two servants for company – Joe Murray, afterwards a faithful favourite of my own, and a sluttish cook from the village known to all as 'Lady Betty', under whose rule of folly the place became a pigsty. It was Joe Murray, more than sixty years old when I took him over with the Abbey, who told me most of what I know about my great-uncle William. Poor old Murray! He was a singularly decrepit creature, and moved more like an unoiled suit of armour than a man. Yet while I knew him I saw him recover twice from diseases that would have killed a troop of horse, and now I believe he promises to bear away the palm of longevity from Old Parr. A great singer of songs ribald and profane in the company of duchesses, Joe Murray. I liked him for this, as for much else, and commissioned a portrait painted of him, which I trust will never leave Newstead even if I have and Murray must. I was, as I say, exceedingly fond of him, and when I dined at Newstead in my later youth, and he stood in attendance behind my chair, it was my pleasure to pass a glass of Bucellas over my shoulder to him, Murray being quite an accomplished toper and partial to that particular white wine.

It is to honest old Murray that I owe yet another piece of family history, and my final story concerning my great-uncle: about the crickets. (Man's a phenomenon, and in nothing more phenomenal than his lusts.) Very well then, ladies and gentlemen, know that my great-uncle the fifth Lord Byron amused himself in his solitude by taming the crickets with which the Abbey swarmed. His chief comfort and diversion and source of sexual solace in his lattermost days was to lie stark naked on the floor of his dressing chamber while these crickets crawled all over his happy body. Why happy? Why because my great-uncle William was a keen student of nature, and knew that crickets like to feast upon aphides, or ant-cows, for their yield of honey-dew; he would therefore paint his testicles with honey-dew, and permit a herd of ant-cows to browse upon his penis, with a consequence that the Newstead crickets congregated in those parts of his anatomy, and concentrated on them with their wings. My great-uncle William was perhaps the first man in the shire of Nottingham ever to achieve emission by stridulation, and as he came (so Murray told me) he even used in his pleasure himself to *chirp*. I trust that there was plenty of this chirping before he died at the age of seventy-six, wife-less, oak-less, and elm-less, attended only by Joe Murray, the Lady Betty, and his crickets. Murray told me that on the night of my great-uncle's passing all the crickets left Newstead Abbey, marching out in such mighty numbers down the long stairs and out through the front door that it was impossible to move an inch without treading on the creatures.

To such a magnificient (if eccentric) predecessor and to such a stumpy inheritance did I succeed. The Abbey when we inspected it was over-run also with cats – ('Better cats than rats,' said Lady Betty) – and I found a sheep's head in my great-uncle William's bedroom cupboard. It soon became evident that there could be no living there in the ancestral home until extensive repairs had been effected. This was of course a sad blow for my mother, since she had come down from Aberdeen with soaring anticipations and ambitions, and after selling all her furniture (as she told the world) for £74 17s and 7d. As for me, I adored everything about Newstead from the moment I clapped eyes upon it, and I signalized my arrival as the sixth Lord Byron by planting an oak tree slap-bang in the middle of the south lawn. My destiny is linked to that oak tree – as it prospers, so do I prosper, and as it fails, so shall I fail, please Zeus. I planted it, of course, in a perfectly unsuitable postion.

Sometimes in my head I still like to wander through the Abbey as I knew it, though now I am talking about Newstead a little later (*circa* 1808, when I started to render my mansion habitable). I was never one for noticing what I believe is called 'interior decoration', but among my souvenirs is a printed inventory (done by Farebrothers of Beaufort Buildings, in the Strand), drawn up for the first intended sale of the place some three years ago;

LOT 131. A very superb (five feet six) double screwed FOUR-POST BEDSTEAD, on French castors; the feet posts carved, and finished in burnished gold; rich pattern FURNITURE, lined with yellow; full green silk and yellow draperies, rich SILK French fringe, gilt cornice, surmounted by a carved coronet, lines, tassels, &c.

That was my bed.

Lot 132. A superb LOFTY double screwed six-feet FOUR-POST BEDSTEAD, on French castors, the pillars japanned and richly gilt, with RICH CRIMSON furniture, folding VELVET and scarlet draperies and valence, with doom top, richly studded, surmounted by a Coronet, and the draperies richly fringed with scarlet and black French fringe, with tassels, &c. supported by carved Eagles, superbly gilt.

And that was my sister Augusta's.

Is it just unpardonable nostalgia that drives me to sit and read this even here in Italy under the oleanders? Young ladies may see me and imagine that I am lost in Dante or Goethe, when in fact the pages I am perusing hold a poetry like this.

I think that's enough about that for now, and more than enough about Newstead.

A letter today from Shelley, written at Milan. He comes here in a week to see me, as he says, about 'a matter of life and death'. I can guess only too easily what this matter will be, but for the moment I prefer not to think about it.

Poor splendid Shelley! Most of those who know only his publications seem to consider him a windy bugbear, but he is (to my knowledge) in fact the least selfish and the *mildest* of men – a man who has made more sacrifice of his fortune and feelings for others than any I ever heard of. I count him the Saint John the Baptist of modern English verse. With his speculative opinions I have nothing in common, nor do I desire to have. An agitated soul, but seraphical, and not lacking courage. I remember two summers ago when the pair of us found ourselves in a gale of wind in a small boat, right under the rocks between Meillerie and St Gingo on the Lake of Geneva. There were five altogether in that boat – a servant, two boatmen, and ourselves. The sail was mismanaged, and the boat was filling fast. Shelley cannot swim. (A poet who worships water, but cannot swim!) I stripped off my coat; then made him strip off his and take hold of an oar, telling him that I thought (being myself an expert swimmer) I could save him if he just held on to the oar and did not struggle. We were then some hundred yards from the rocks, with an awkward swell running. 'You hear me?' I cried. Shelley smiled and shook his head. 'Are you deaf or mad?' I shouted. Then Shelley remarked with the greatest possible coolness and politeness that he had no least notion of being saved, and that in his view I would have sufficient to do to try to save myself. I persisted. He thanked me, but declined all my offers of assistance. Nor did he make any large statements about either death or destiny, which if anything impressed me even more. He just sat there smiling. Luckily, the boat righted, and, baling, we got round the point and into St Gingo, where the inhabitants came down and embraced the boatmen on their narrow escape, the wind having been high enough to tear up some huge trees from the Alps above us, as we saw the next day. Yet this same Shelley, who struck me as being as cool and collected as it is possible to be in such circumstances (of which I am no judge myself, since the knowledge that one can swim quite naturally gives a certain self-possession when near shore, no matter if your boat is sinking) – this same Shelley once fainted clean away in my company, his fevered imagination having pictured to him eyes in place of nipples in the bosom of his wife.

CHAPTER FOUR

I Fall Three Times in Love, and Lose the Rest of my Virginity

My little girl Allegra (my natural daughter) came with me this afternoon in my gondola while I went swanning about the archipelago to choose a spot for my grave. My notion is to plant a weeping willow and be buried under it. The branches of such a tree, drooping over the waters, will provide a fitting shadow for my tomb, erected here under the azure sky of the South, close to Heaven and the Adriatic. As for an epitaph, I saw some recently that pleased me more than all the splendid monuments of Rome; for instance –

'Martini Luigi
Implora pace.'
'Lucrezia Picini
Implora eterna quiete.'

Could anything be more full of pathos? Those few words say all that can be said or sought. The dead had had enough of life; all they wanted was rest; and this they '*implore*'. There you have all the helplessness and humble hope and deathlike prayer that can arise from the grave: '*implore pace*'. I hope, whoever may survive me and shall see me put in the foreigners' burying-ground at the Lido will have those two words and no more put over me.

But not quite yet.

As a general principle, I should admit that I abominate the sight of children so much that I have always had the greatest respect for the character of Herod. But Allegra has been with me here in Venice for nearly three months now, and I begin to make her the exception that proves the rule. She is a pretty child, intelligent and clean, and a great favourite with everybody, from my gondolier to my monkeys. It was Shelley's scheme that she come to live with me. Yet her mother, his sister-in-law, that damned bitch Claire Clairmont (never trust a woman whose name repeats itself), wrote just this morning with the perfectly lunatic suggestion that I should now consign the infant back to him. I have fired off an immediate answer, refusing point-blank, telling her that in my opinion to do something like that would be like committing a healthy soul to a hospital full of contagious diseases. The Shelleys, after all, have never succeeded in *rearing* a single brat, though they have spawned several. Little Allegra's health while in my household has been excellent, and her temper not bad. She is sometimes vain and obstinate, but always cheerful. In a year or two, I shall probably post her to England, or put her into a convent here for education, and then these defects will be remedied as far as they can ever be in human nature. But the child shall certainly not quit me again in order to perish of idealism and green fruit at the Shelleys, or to be pumped full of hot air and taught by them that there is no Deity and that poets are the unacknowledged legislators of the world. Poets are nothing of the sort, for which we must thank God or Plato. I fear Shelley is quite mad on the subject of the importance of what some of us do to relieve ourselves with our right hand and some ink. As for me, I have never ranked poetry high in the scale of intelligence. (This may look like affectation, but it is my real opinion.) I would claim that poetry is the lava of the imagination whose eruption prevents an earthquake, that is all; and we should draw no laws, acknowledged or otherwise, from the way the lava flows. Shelley won't see this; the less Shelley he! I can never get people to understand that poetry is the expression of *excited passion*, and that there is no such thing as a life of passion any more than a continuous earthquake, or an eternal fever. Besides, who would ever *shave* themselves in such a state?

This old house smells of rot, like all of Venice. It also smells of animals, but that's like nothing (or everything) on earth. Tonight I'm writing in the music-room. If I say a word out aloud it floats up to the vaulted roof, and echoes there. '*Shelley*,' I say. '*Allegra*,' I say. '*Augusta*.' I like these names. Yet all our names are nothing.

Sitting face-to-face with Allegra in that gondola today, confirmed a general impression formed before but never quite specifically admitted. She is much more like my wife than she is like her mother – so much so as to stupefy my valet Fletcher, who simply refuses to believe that she can be La Clairmont's child. The resemblance to Lady Byron astonishes and a little dismays me. It is odd. I suppose the girl must also resemble her half-sister Ada. But it is more than two years now since I saw Ada, and she was at that time too young and small to do much more than resemble a monkey, which in my opinion is what we all do in extreme infancy as well as extreme old age. Very blue eyes, a singular forehead, fair curly hair: this is Allegra. She has a devil of a spirit too, but that is Papa's.

I loved before I understood the name or the meaning of love. The love of Dante for Beatrice was a passion of this kind – the child whom he saw smiling in her infancy, crowned in her girlhood with a death garland, and afterwards by the stars of heaven. The name of my Beatrice was Mary Duff, my cousin and my first of flames at the age of eight. We were both the merest children yet I swear that our passion was not the less for it. My mother laughed at me, the parents of the girl and the friends of both our houses ridiculed us, but I continued to love my Beatrice sadly and seriously, with all the tenderness and purity of childhood. I recollect all that we said to each other, all our caresses, her features, my restlessness, sleeplessness, my tormenting my mother's maid to write notes for me to my beloved, which she at last did, to quiet me. Poor Nancy thought I was mad, and, as I could not write adequately for myself, became my secretary. I remember, too, our walks, and the sheer happiness of sitting by my Mary, in the children's apartment, at her parents' house not far from the Plain-stanes at Aberdeen, while her lesser sister Helen played with a shiny china doll, and we sat gravely making love, in our childish fashion.

Fate parted us, whom time had never joined for long. Then, when I was sixteen, and learned that my Beatrice was to be married, the news nearly threw me into convulsions. Why? Our greatest passions are for women unpossessed, but remember in this case that we were both children. I really cannot explain or account for my feelings. Dante would have understood, perhaps.

I have been thinking lately a great deal again of this Mary Duff. How very odd it is that I should have been so utterly, so devotedly fond of that girl, and at such an impossible age. My love for her was so violent, in fact, that I sometimes doubt if I have ever been truly as attached or attracted since. How divinely pretty is the perfect image of her which I hold still in my memory – her dark brown hair, parted in the middle; her hazel eyes; her very dress! I should be quite grieved and dismayed to see her *now*, that I am sure of. The reality, however beautiful, would destroy, or at least confuse, the features of the lovely Peri which then existed in her, and lives still in the most holy chamber of my imagination, at the distance of more than twenty years.

No doubt in a body as vigorous, a character as energetic, and an imagination as exalted (not to say fevered) as mine, this early development of love was a natural occurrence. In the first years of youth one loves unconsciously, and before the instincts of nature are fully awakened; then, later on, when we experience a profound passion, we know that we have loved blindly before. Be that as it may, at eleven I was smitten a second time, this time with the sweet charms of another young cousin of mine, called Margaret Parker. She was in fact a first cousin, so I was progressing. She was also the inspiration for my second dash into poetry, and one of the most beautiful of evanescent beings. (My first lines had been penned at the age of nine – an outburst of rhyme against an old woman I detested: it was rage that started the poet in me.) I have long forgotten the verses I wrote about Margaret Parker, but it would be difficult for me to forget her. Those dark eyes, as black as Death! Those long eye-lashes, the same hue! That completely Greek cast of face and figure, with a short upper lip and a body fit for the model of a statuary! This same Margaret, but one year my elder, died only a year after I first met her, in consequence of a fall downstairs which injured her spine and induced a consumption. I knew nothing of her illness (being at Harrow and in the country), till she was gone. Some years later, I made an attempt at an elegy. A very dull one, spoiled by too much feeling and not enough technique. I do not recollect scarcely anything equal to the *transparent* beauty of my cousin, or to the honey sweetness of her temper during the short period of our intimacy. She looked as if she had been made out of a rainbow – all beauty and peace. My passion had its usual effects upon me: I could not sleep, could not eat; I could not rest; and although I had reason to know that Margaret loved me, it was the torture of my life to think of the time which must elapse before we could meet again – being usually about *twelve hours* of separation, which seemed to me then all I would ever need to know about eternity! But I was a fool in those days, and am not much wiser now.

I was fifteen before I fell in love for the third time. It happened then that the unfortunate dear object of my affections was a whole two years my senior, yet despite this (as you might suppose) evidence of an increasing interest in maturity on my part, the attack was so severe that I refused to return to Harrow for the entire autumn term of 1803, spending instead every possible moment that I could with my beloved. Her name was Mary Chaworth, and she was a great niece of the Mr Chaworth impaled by my uncle William in the duel in the locked room. The fact that a corpse lay between our hearts and that this made us somewhat of a Romeo and Juliet was not lost upon me. Mary Chaworth! The very air seemed lighter from her eyes! She was the *beau ideal* of all that my youthful fancy could paint of the beautiful, and I have taken most of my fables about the celestial nature of women from the perfection my imagination created in her – I say *created* and mean it, for alas I found her, in the end, like the rest of her sex, something less than an angel. And yet, in the early days of our acquaintance, there were moments when I felt that it would not be idolatry to kneel in her presence. As this will no doubt suggest, it was from the start a thoroughly one-sided attachment. The ardour was all on my side. I was serious, she was volatile. She liked me as a younger brother, and treated me and laughed at me as a boy. She never took me seriously as a suitor. She was, in fact, engaged, during the latter part of the time I adored her, at least, to one Jack Munsters, a foul-breathed, fox-hunting fool who proved to be a bad, faithless, and unkind husband to her. The high moment in her relations with me came late one summer night, at Annesley Hall, her family home, when she did not know that I was standing below her in a turn of the stairs, and I overheard her maid-servant asking her if she was in love with me, and I heard her laugh and say, 'What, do you think I could feel anything for that lame boy?' The sentence was like a shot clean through my heart. I plunged straight out of the house and into the night, and scarcely knowing where I ran, never stopped till I found myself back at Newstead. Next morning, though, I returned, yet never mentioned to her what I had heard her say. I remember going with her to a ball at Matlock where she danced with many partners while I leaned against a pillar, always unable to dance of course on account of my foot. While she waltzed I put my hands over my heart, fearing that its violent drum-drum-drum might be heard through the saloons. I remember also going with her one summer's day to Derbyshire to see some grottoes underground. We had to cross in a boat an inky stream which flows under a lintel of rock, with the rock so close upon the water as to admit the boat only to be pushed on by a ferryman (a sort of Charon) who waded at the stern, stooping all the time, while Mary and I lay pressed together in the bottom of the boat. She observed that my body trembled as I lay next to her, and remarked aloud upon it. I told her that it was not from fear. Whether she understood, I do not know. I can still recollect my sensations, but I cannot now describe them, and it is as well.

For a while after my experience of Mary Chaworth I was so unsure of myself in the presence of any woman that on being introduced to a member of the sex I found it necessary to count under my breath up to seven before speaking or acting further. I could wish sometimes that I had never grown out of that habit.

I suppose that before concluding this chapter about the early affections and infections of my heart, I had better set down something about how I was raped. This momentous event occurred when I was still a schoolboy at Harrow, but it was not one of my school-fellows nor even one of the masters who was to blame. I had come home to Newstead for my holidays, only to find that the usual financial necessity had obliged my dear mamma to let the place to Lord Grey de Ruthyn, a nasty red-headed sort of scoundrel, aged twenty-three or four, a great shooter of pellets at pheasants and sharper of cards at bridge. When he was not cheating my mother at the latter game, he spent a deal of time insolently paying court to her as if enamoured of her gross beauty. My foolish mother was much flattered. As for me, I saw straight through his bowings and jokings, his amblings with her round and round the lake as still and cold as Southey's eye, his mysterious silences and his even more mysterious protestations that she was the nearest thing to Juno he had ever adored or desired. Lord Grey de Ruthyn was in fact as queer as a coot – though quite why that poor web-foot bird should always be dragged in as the paragon of pathics, I have never understood. Reader, let us be frank. It was not my mother's declivities this Lord Grey was after, but her property. And so, since I was part of that property at the time, as well as being desirably male, and a boy of some innocence (albeit tattered), the lusty vulgar villain soon enough saw fit to come after me. One night, after I had been persuaded out of boredom to accompany him all afternoon around the tree-stumps while he cocked his rifle at the pheasants and the partridges and missed, he soaped himself in a big brown wooden tub in front of the fire, encouraged me to join him in some slices of red meat and two bottles of Madeira wine, and then finished off his day's sport by attempting to bugger me on the hearth-rug. I was exceeding drunk, but not that drunk, and contrived without much difficulty to pass a turd and dislodge him before he spent. I remember his rusty hirsute armpits and his balls and phallus like something off a bull. He came all over the fire-irons. 'Forgive me, sir,' I said, 'if your pleasure was marred.' It was his manners rather than his morals which I detested. However, I said nothing to my mother nor to anyone else, save that I warned the poor silly woman that in my opinion her new beau would not make the best of husbands. As to why I told no one, it was not out of shame, nor because I ever desired anything save never to find myself within pissing or shitting distance of Lord Grey de Ruthyn again, but simply because in English law sodomy is a hanging matter, and though I had cause I had no great wish to see the bugger hung.

CHAPTER FIVE

I Begin in the Abominable Trade of Versifying

My sister Augusta always used to say that she could not abide books that had no conversations in them. So here is a brief specimen of the art: a conversation which I had this morning with Allegra.

'Did you sleep well, Papa?' she said.

'Six hours,' I said. 'But I had a dream.'

'Was it the same dream you had last week?' she said.

'No, child,' I said. 'It was a new dream.'

'Are dreams from God?' Allegra said.

'Oh yes,' I said. 'Dreams are a godsend.'

'Then we must believe them,' Allegra said.

The sweetness of her simplicity puts me to shame. Is it Aquinas or Augustine who speaks of certain *natural* Christian souls? children who, from their birth, have an innate capacity for faith? Despite her parentage (begotten by despair upon impossibility, as Citizen Marvell would have said), my daughter Allegra seems to me one of these shining ones, even allowing for her addiction to rude songs and Turkish delight.

Later, I was feeding my magpie in the pantry when Allegra came up again and said, 'Tell me your dream, Papa.'

'Well,' I said, 'I dreamt I was walking by deep waters and a leaf fell into my hand. I laid the leaf among the reeds and the waters swallowed it with a snap.'

'Is that all?' asked Allegra.

'That's all,' I said.

'A good dream,' said Allegra. Then she added, 'It could have been a fish.'

'No, child,' I said. 'It wasn't a fish.'

'A crab then?' said Allegra.

It was on the tip of my tongue to declare that a man of my experience knows a crustacean when he sees one, but I laughed instead, and took her on my knee. 'I withdraw my dream,' I said. 'I saw the water snap. It was the best part of the dream. I should like to keep it.'

'You don't dream properly, Papa,' Allegra said. 'You never get it right.'

'In the telling?' I said.

'No,' said Allegra. 'In the dreaming.'

No doubt my daughter's criticism is just, and Gifford of the *Quarterly* would agree with her. Still, I say that there are more things in this good round world than are philosophised out of dreaming. I have never been as keen on nightmares and visions as some of my contemporaries are. Let us make the most of life, I say, and leave dreams to Emanuel Swedenborg.

Of course I occupy myself setting down all this charming nonsense because I have other (I will not say more important but assuredly more difficult) matters which I am avoiding. Having spoken freely, you see, of certain minor loves, I hesitate now to say anything at all of one unquestionably major and certainly much deeper and darker in my heart. There are things which out of regard for the living may barely be mentioned. Yet not to mention them must mean that I write in too much detail of that which interests me least – so that my autobiographical essay resembles the tragedy of *Hamlet* at the country theatre, recited 'with the part of the Prince left out by popular demand'. I do not see any simple way round this. Fortunately, for the moment I can postpone thinking about the problem, since in the period of which I am still writing this passion had not yet arisen to vex and bless my existence. But I can see that, like Allegra with her alphabet, I shall have to confront it without blinking before long.

In the Easter holidays of 1804 began that part of my life which I mis-spent with my mother in the small (but to me vastly annoying) town of Southwell, in the county of Notts. Newstead being impossible save for short summer visits, and infested even then by her unpleasant tenant Lord Grey de Ruthyn, whose unsuitability as a suitor was now recognised, she had withdrawn with me for a brief time to Nottingham itself. There is nothing to record of the Nottingham days beyond the fact that the final efforts to 'cure' my afflicted foot were made in them. This was the work of a quack named Lavender, whose treatment consisted of sitting on my leg and twisting my ankle, and then screwing it neatly and assiduously into shape between two thick planks of polished cedar wood. When these tortures were completed without any improvement in my condition, my mother settled for having a special pair of boots made for me by a medical cobbler called Sheldrake.

In ill-favoured Southwell my mother took for us a house called Burgage Manor, situated by the side of the

Green. Our life there was less than happy, owing chiefly to a recurrence of those fearful outbursts of temper which came as naturally to my mamma as storms to the bay of Cadiz. It is true that I made matters worse during her paroxysms by assuming an expression of polite interest and offering exaggerated low bows all the time in response to her tirades against the '*Byrrones*'. (She made our family name sound like a disease of the spleen or a race of trolls – which, indeed, now I come to reflect upon it, is perhaps after all not so wide of the mark.) Then in her fury my mother would hurl crockery and pokers at my person, while I dodged round the furniture like a will o' the wisp in surgical boots.

Still, if these Southwell days had their miseries they had also their own eager interest. That December, Napoleon was crowned Emperor in Paris. And Telford commenced his construction of the Caledonian Canal. And it was in this period, in that aforesaid unpropitious place, and in the company of a most unlikely maternal Muse, that my first sustained essays in authorship were undertaken. I had written verses at Harrow, as I believe I have already confessed, and on one or two other isolated love-sick occasions, but now the vice began to establish a definite hold upon me. Much to my mother's eloquent alarm, I became quite industrious with the pen and developed certain habits to which I have adhered ever since, namely sitting up to write late into the night and making up for that by lying in bed the whole morning next day, a shocking let-down to the wisdom that associates early rising with health and wealth, not to speak of the catching of worms. (Let us on no account speak of the catching of worms.) My tendency to this excellent mode of life is in fact constitutional, since I am always suicidal in my feelings when I get up, so choose to get up at or after midday on the very good grounds that the afternoon is no time for suicide.

Of course sometimes I woke up early in those days, and there was then the awful problem of what to do with the morning. I solved this at Southwell by the cultivation of a mild mania for arms. On the opposite side of the Green was the home of a family named Pigot, with whose younger members I became friendly. Sometimes I think these Pigots were the only ordinary decent folk I have ever known in my whole life. (Though such a judgement, partaking of melodrama, says more about me than about them.) Eliza Pigot used to read aloud to me from Burns while I ate grapes upon a sofa. Her brother John, a student doctor, collected swords. I borrowed from him a small sword of Toledo steel which took my fancy, and on mornings when I awoke too early and the necessity for amusement arose I used to lie in bed thrusting this sword in and out of my bed curtains. That eccentric habit, undesirable though it might be from a general point of view, did not prove so unfavourable to my mother as might have been expected, for when, on leaving Southwell for Newstead, she sold such of the furniture as belonged to her, the price fetched by my bed was a great deal higher than would have been the case if the hangings had been in a better condition, the lady who purchased it labouring under the misapprehension that the damage had been wrought with the very sword used in the Chaworth duel. No doubt she got full value for the extra outlay from the shudders with which she would exhibit, and her friends inspect, the supposed gruesome relic.

However, as I was trying just now to say, the chief circumstance which lends interest to my time in Southwell is that it was then and there that I first began to give myself up to what my dear wife once called 'the abominable trade of versifying'. I should admit that in those days, being young and foolish, I had altogether a higher opinion of poetry and poets than is now the case, although I was never at any stage of my life a great *reader* of the stuff. The mighty stir made about scribbling and scribes, by themselves and others, seems to me now a sign of effeminacy, degeneracy, and weakness. Who would write who had anything better to do? These days, being old and perhaps less foolish, I have no great esteem for the pursuit of poetry. In fact, I have just this moment thrown a poem into the fire (which it has relighted to my comfort). Yet I would still be fair to my younger self, and in all fairness then I must confess that my younger self was always more than half in love with the idea of poetical fame. As to my older self and what its fame has achieved, I think I may dare say that no one has done more through negligence to corrupt the language. I versified to some extent since I was fourteen years old, but it was now, at dreadful Southwell, a suburb of Hell, under the genial influence of Eliza Pigot's encouragement, that the Muse first took possession of my vacant mind. A fat and bashful boy, I soon had enough matter to hand for a thin bad volume.

The history of that small first volume of mine is very brief and a little pathetic. It was intended for private circulation only, and was printed by S. and J. Ridge, of Newark, who had, I fear, a trying experience by reason of the corrections, additions, second thoughts, emendations, and so forth, which were continually fired in their direction by the anxious author. The venture was begun in August 1806 and finished by November, a little quarto volume of thirty-eight poems occupying sixty-six pages, entitled *Fugitive Pieces*. Then I sat down to the agreeable task of sending off the first presentation copies. The favoured recipients were my friends the Pigots and a clergyman acquaintance, the Rev. John Thomas Becher, vicar of Rympton. I respected Becher, with his caustic eyes and his nose like a turnip and his habit of stroking his pale moustache with the fingernail of his right thumb while he thought about anything that had been said to him. This little carbuncular clergyman had been kind to me. Even in those days my private opinions regarding religion were hardly orthodox, yet he scolded me for this in the most amiable and tolerant manner. I remember on one occasion he strove to convince me over a particularly third-rate claret that the Providence against which I railed and grumbled had in fact dowered me with a rich diversity of boons – with rank, wit, a fortune (very shortly), and above all with (he said) 'a mind which places you above the rest of mankind'. At which I placed my finger on my brow and said, 'If *this* places me above the rest of mankind, *that*' – and I pointed to my foot – 'places me far, far below them.' Anyway, to cut short a scarcely long story, among these precious *juvenilia* of mine was one poem, entitled *To Mary*, which shocked to the blessed roots my friend the clergyman. He wrote to me immediately on receipt of my book, in terms of generous and judicious expostulation, all neatly rhymed, begging me not to allow this first-born to see more of the light. He asked a hard thing, but I heeded him. That evening I committed the whole edition (with the exception of the two copies already given) to the flames. Whether the Pigots' copy is still extant, I do not know. Becher's most certainly is not. I am pleased also to be able to report that the verses which had been objected to as 'too warmly drawn' are now erased from my own memory quite, with the exception of one phrase concerning 'love's extatic posture' which had especially arrested the attention of the Rev. John Thomas. I am sure that there was nothing to compensate for their silly viciousness – not one felicity of thought or expression.

So ended (in appropriate flames) my first venture into print; but it was swiftly followed by a second, for *Poems on Various Occasions*, a somewhat larger volume than its predecessor, and, like it, printed for private circulation and anonymously, appeared the following January (1807). And then, in that same year, my nineteenth, came the first real plunge with *Hours of Idleness*, this time for the public at large. For a man to become a poet (witness Petrarch and Dante, not to speak of Stephen Duck), he must be in love, or miserable. I was both when I wrote *Hours of Idleness*, but not perhaps enough, or too much. The volume's printer was still Ridge, of Newark, but this time it was sold by three or four London booksellers, and was not anonymous, but bore on the title-page the imposing and (I now think) ridiculous (if accurate) inscription, 'By George Gordon, Lord Byron, a Minor'. And the public at large read my book – those of them who were not too busy along the south coast of England making preparations against the expected invasion by Napoleon.

Napoleon never came, but I may say *I did*. In other words, I was soon a man (or at any rate, a Major) whose works were praised by reviewers, admired by duchesses, and sold by every bookseller of the Metropolis. In short, some species of that odd flower: poet. I would rather have been something else, but perhaps there is nothing else that I could have been. If I didn't write to empty my mind, I should go mad no doubt. But as to what some call a 'love of writing', I do not understand it. I feel it as a torture, which I must get rid of, but never as a pleasure. On the contrary, I consider composition a great pain.

Tonight as I returned from the Lido we were overtaken by one of the summer storms that strike as swift as lightning in these parts. The gondola was put in peril – hats blown away, boat filling, oar lost, tumbling sea, thunder, rain in torrents, night coming, and wind increasing. On our return, after a tight struggle, I found Margarita awaiting me on the steps of the palazzo, with her great black eyes flashing through her tears, and the long dark hair, which was streaming, drenched with rain, over her brows and breast. The wind blowing her hair and dress about her tall thin figure, and the lightning flashing round her, with the waves rolling at her feet, made her look like Medea alighted from her chariot, or the sibyl of the tempest. On seeing me safe, she did not wait to greet me, but called out, *'Ah! can' della Madonna, xe esto il tempo per andar' al' Lido?'* (Ah! Dog of the Virgin, is this a time to go to the Lido?) and ran into the house, and solaced herself with scolding the servants. Truth to tell, my valet, the learned Fletcher, is terrified of the creature. Her joy tonight at seeing me survive the storm was moderately mixed with ferocity, and gave me the idea of a tigress over her recovered cubs. She had me tool her on the billiard table, then on the marble staircase, a third time hard up against the cage where I keep my wolf.

CHAPTER SIX

I Proceed to Cambridge, Where I Keep a Bear

Alas, my masters, here's a pretty plot. Shelley came two days ago, as threatened. The same strange Shelley, he never changes – tall, gangling, hair standing up as if he has just this minute given himself an electric shock, pale but blushing crimson at any embarrassment, talking nineteen to the dozen even as he dashes two steps a time up the stairs of the palazzo to greet me, a book of Greek verse in his left hand, that shrill familiar laugh like the scream of a peacock, eyes like blue bonfires of saints' bones, red lips always slightly agape, the awkward stumbling *rush* and peculiar baby-powderish *smell* of him, that pea-green schoolboy jacket a size too small and his silly sailor trousers flaring out at the ankles. 'Albé!' he cried, and then, falling forwards, he kissed me. I recoiled from that kiss. I was right. There was Judas in it.

We took tea, with toast and honey, on the terrace. My friend loves tea, and, for a transcendentalist, makes very quick work of his toast. We talked as we sat there of what we always talk about: that is, of God, of truth, of destiny, of free will. But I knew all the time that it was nothing to do with any of this which had brought him here. He knows, after all, my opinions on these matters, and I know his, and we agree to differ. He believes in the perfectibility of man, and I believe I am a martyr to women. He believes in Good and Evil; I deny nothing, but doubt everything. He believes in Utopia, and I believe in Venice. (A most specific item of my creed, incidentally, is that the women of Venice *kiss* better than those of any other nation, a notorious fact which none can dispute, to be attributed to the worship of images and the early habit of osculation induced thereby.) And – lest I should be dismissed as merely facetious in these comparisons – may I add that as I sat there on the terrace listening to Shelley spout (which verb I use although I love him dearly), as I sat there a very serious and dreadful thought came into my head, which thought was that though he is truth and honour itself and a very fine poet there are moments when he resembles too closely for comfort a Methodist preacher I once endured with my mother, who on perceiving a profane grin on the faces of part of his congregation, exclaimed in a great roar: '*No hope for them as laughs!*'

Well, I'm not laughing now. Here's why.

'How's Allegra?' said Shelley.

'Very well,' I answered.

'Her mother's worried,' said Shelley.

'She's a worrying woman,' I said.

Shelley was licking honey from his fingers, more from embarrassment (I think) than any greed. 'I suppose there is no chance at all that you and Claire—'

I cut him short. 'Shelley, you're talking nonsense. I never loved Claire, or even pretended to love her. But a man is a man, and if a girl of eighteen comes prancing to you at all hours. . . .'

There was a little difficult silence between us. Then I said: 'And thus people come into the world.'

'Allegra,' he said.

'Allegra,' I said.

'Byron, Claire wants her back again,' he said.

'I cannot agree to that at all,' I said. 'The child is not a shuttlecock in some game. Claire has relinquished her once. Damn it, she *wanted* me to take Allegra off her hands. Allegra is happy here, and I have grown fond of her. Why don't you ask her yourself?'

'Byron, Claire wants to see her,' he said.

I smiled, and nodded. I guessed instantly that he had not journeyed alone to Venice, that Claire was with him at his hotel, but I said nothing. 'Under the present arrangements,' I said, 'Claire is free to see Allegra from time to time, so long as I do not have to see Claire at any time.'

'Byron, why not let Allegra live with me and Mary?' Shelley said.

I pointed out politely that Claire herself had already proposed this to me, and I had rejected it, and my friend stared gloomily at a passing gondola, blushing even more violently than usual, so that I was able silently to pity him for the mighty poor conspirator his wife and his sister-in-law have made of him. That pity was the undoing of my pride. Shelley detected it, and the intuition gave him the excuse he had been seeking. All at once, stammering but eloquent, he launched into a long palaver about lawyers and La Clairmont; about stories Claire had collected concerning the comings and goings of my mistresses here at the Mocenigo; about how Allegra's nursemaid, a Swiss miss, had gone to the wife of the British Consul in Venice, Mrs Hoppner, herself a Switzer, and enlisted this stout lady's help in insisting that proceedings be set in hand to separate my natural daughter from her unnatural father. It was a very ugly speech, and Shelley knew it, especially one phrase about the 'immoral prison' of my house.

When he'd finished, I offered him an orange.

'Be serious, Byron,' he said, and threw it into the canal.

So I was serious. I did not have much choice. I said that if possible I think even less of La Clairmont now that she is doing her best to deny me even the prospect of a little happiness with my darling daughter as the pillar of my old age. I said that on the other hand I was capable of taking three steps back from my own desires and wishes, and admitting then that perhaps it might not be *sensible* for Allegra to remain in this *ménage* (or should I say menagerie?) of mine. I said that I thought the main thing was to do what was best for Allegra. On no account should the child be torn apart by the hate between me and Claire. To that end, after much lip-twisting and nail-biting, I suggested that I would arrange for Allegra to be boarded in the best convent I could find, where she could be educated, where both her parents could visit her separately, and from which she would be able to visit them.

Fifteen minutes of high-minded abuse of the Roman Catholic Church followed from Shelley, supplemented with an exposition of the doctrine of someone called Intellectual Beauty. While this went on – and in order to stop myself from weeping as I wished – I entertained my imagination with daydreams of what a pretty fight would ensue if the bitch Claire should ever dare turn up here and encounter Margarita.

But I'm really too choked with despair and anger and disgust to write very much more about this. Finally, then, suffice it to say that (as I believe often happens in such cases in real life, not to mention novels) *a compromise* was reached. My dearest Allegra and her damned Swiss nurse are to be boarded, indefinitely, at my expense, with the British Consul Mr Richard Hoppner and his good Swiss spouse. Allegra is to be free to come to stay with me whenever she wants to, and for as long as she likes. Her mother to have the same privileges.

'Byron, I am sure that this will all be for the best,' Shelley said, when our melancholy business was concluded. I said nothing. I was watching Allegra down on the steps of the palazzo where she played with a paper boat. But I have my spies and tale-tellers too, and I heard that the same evening Shelley gave it as his opinion that the new arrangements will leave Lord Byron the more free to spend his time with Italian ladies who smell so strongly of garlic that an ordinary Englishman would prefer not to approach them, as well as with (and I quote) 'wretches who seem almost to have lost the gait and physiognomy of man, and who do not scruple to avow practices which are not only not named but I believe not even conceived in England.' To which I say only: Since when was Shelley 'an ordinary Englishman'? And can he really be so innocent or ignorant regarding what is not only known and conceived but done at least a thousand times a day by those who are not-Shelleys in England?

As a matter of fact, I could almost believe that Shelley is now in love with Claire, and if so it is at least possible that some of this confusion is my fault; something instructs me that he would not love her if I did, that he feels he must love her because I cannot. Southey once put it about that Shelley and Mary, Claire and I, all lived together at Geneva those years ago in 'a League of Incest'. I hate him as much for that lie as for his stupid verses. Claire was the only one I slept with, and that not often, our intercourse being more her doing than is commonly the case in my affairs.

But if Shelley is now sleeping with his sister-in-law as well as with Mary, I have a horrid suspicion that this is at least partly because he has never slept with me. How complicated and unpleasant, the human heart! My little Allegra is well out of it, at the Hoppners', especially as Margarita gave her too many sweetmeats. So my dear daughter has been released from what her mother calls 'the immoral prison' of my company.

My release from the moral prison that was Southwell came in June, 1807, when I was nineteen. I always hated the place, and spent as much time as I did in it only from necessity. The fact is, I remained there because I could appear nowhere else, being completely done up. Wine and women dished me in those early days, and there was not a *sou* to be had. Thus was I condemned to exist (I cannot say live) in that crater of dullness until my lease of infancy expired. Once that happened I hardly looked back to wonder how it was that I had ever tolerated existence there. To forget and be forgotten by the people of Southwell is all that I still aspire to. Yet those Pigots I liked. Sometimes I wonder how their lives have turned out since, and what they might think of mine.

I had been enrolled as an undergraduate at Cambridge since October, 1805, so that was my status when my first incursions into print were made. In the meantime, I daresay I had been cultivating a somewhat inflated opinion of myself and my works. So it was as well – indeed, probably it could be said to have been an excellent thing for me from every point of view – that there now came a sudden and severe exception to the general adulation which had been otherwise mine, and with which I was (truth to tell) very nearly bored to death. Who it was that wrote the critique of *Hours of Idleness* in the *Edinburgh Review* I am still not certain. It was probably Lord Brougham, whom I had cause enough to hate later for his malice towards me during my separation from my wife, but it has also crossed my mind sometimes that it might equally well have been some Cambridge don piqued into literary criticism by the one or two irreverent remarks about the University and its authorities which my book contained. That article, after all, was just the sort of high-flown mugging which a Cambridge don with piles could perpetrate to perfection. Whoever it was, the villain never yet came forward publicly to claim his laurels. He poured molten lead upon my cradle. Never was criticism so harsh, so implacable. The youthful aspirant to the temple of the Muses, I was told, did not even reach mediocrity. According to this critic, my ideas neither rose nor fell to the same level – they resembled stagnant water. I excused myself, indeed, by speaking of my youth, and this minority was too plainly visible from the beginning to the end of the work as the inseparable companion of my style. I happened, like most other people, to write a great many miserable verses in the interval between leaving school and leaving the university. I should have remembered, however, that to be a poet a little sentiment is necessary, and also a little imagination. My imitations of Ossian and Homer would not pass as good exercises in a class of rhetoric, and were unworthy of publication. In short, the critic boldly declared that the young nobleman was not born to be a poet, and he ought therefore to leave this enchanting art to those of taste and talent.

The effect upon the young nobleman was that of a spur. I replied to that attack with what is perhaps my first work of real note, though I now regret it – I mean my little satire *English Bards and Scotch Reviewers*.

I do the dirty criticaster of the *Edinburgh Review* too much honour, though, if I imply that he was my total inspiration. In fact some 380 lines of my poem had already been written when his attack appeared, so perhaps I should be quite candid and confess that his goadings only had the effect of turning my full energies into this particular channel. A good many couplets were added to the work, and you can well believe that the points and edges of some of those already penned received a sharpening and a dousing in acid. (It occurred to me for the first time about then that Barabbas was a publisher and Pontius Pilate a reviewer.) But if I say that my response was *prompt*, the word must not be understood as involving the haste which might be expected to be attendant upon it. After the first inward turmoil – a friend coming in just as I finished reading the review believed that I must have received a challenge to a duel, and I recall drinking three bottles of claret that evening after dinner – once this spin passed, I determined to hit back with all the care and force the occasion called for. I had been knocked down, but now I got up again fighting. Cawthorne was my publisher (a London house this time), and the success was swift. There is nothing like filling a book with the names of living celebrities in connection with more or less libellous matter to ensure its sale, and in this case I think I may say that the work itself bore witness to the spirit of its author. My mind and my spleen were in it, whereas the earlier productions had accommodated only half my heart. *English Bards and Scotch Reviewers* set half London laughing at the other half, and all Edinburgh wailing. Though the volume had been published anonymously, my identity was generally guessed.

But this was a success dearly purchased, and before long the bill came in. What I mean to say is that quite soon afterwards I became friendly with several of those whom I had attacked, and this made things uncomfortable at the best, and filled me with genuine remorse at the worst. (As a general rule, it is sensible for an author to dine with as few other authors as possible, and ideal if he can confine his company to the dead.) After four small editions had been sold, I did my damndest to suppress the book. I now refuse to countenance the republication of what is still in my opinion a fair poem but, at the same time, a miserable record of misplaced anger and indiscriminate acrimony.

While all this transpired, I had been up and down at Cambridge, that conspiracy of a place designed to put excessive flesh on a man's bones and idleness in his heart. My rooms were in Neville's Court, Trinity, in what was known as Muttonhall Corner. At Cambridge my career was a mixture of severe simplicity and reckless dissipation, or severe dissipation and reckless simplicity, depending on how you look at it. With an old schoolfellow from Harrow, Ned Long, I spent much of my time in swimming and diving – we used to compete at retrieving plates and shillings from a pool some fourteen feet deep – reading, especially the poems of Tom Moore, and music, Long being the performer on violoncello or flute, and I the audience. On all these occasions our chief beverage was soda-water, a drink which has been a trusty stand-by during a large part of my life, and which I am quaffing even now with my left hand while I scribble these words with my right.

At this time I declared myself a Deist destined never to be happy, wore a red Milanese kerchief, and cultivated a romantic and sentimental friendship with a chorister, John Edleston, two years younger than myself, nearly my own height (five feet eight inches), thin as a reed, with a fine voice. A curious circumstance it was that we shared the same birthday, this golden lad and myself, even to the hour. No doubt I saw in him my own likeness improved as in a true and well-framed glass. He was my almost constant companion for about a year. His voice first attracted my attention, his countenance fixed it, and his manners then attached me to him for ever. We used to ride together out to Grantchester of a morning, and go swimming in the Trumpington millpond. On one occasion I suppose I could be said to have saved him from drowning in that pond. He made me a gift of a small carnelian heart and I wrote a set of verses too swollen by affection in which I called him 'Thyrza', taking the name from Gessner's *Abel*. If he had been a girl I would have worshipped him. As it was, our friendship was passionate but pure, almost poetic. The poor sweet-singing fellow died very young of a consumption.

Among my other Cambridge familiars first and foremost stands John Cam Hobhouse, my good friend Hobby. Hobhouse disliked me intensely at first, only opening the yolk which passes for a mouth in his fried egg of a face to object to my white hat, my grey coat, my black horse, my Milanese kerchief, and everything about me, and regarding me (so he told me later) as an arrant coxcomb. I regarded (and regard) him as a very decent slug. It was the publication of the fairly atrocious *Hours of Idleness* which made Hobby blink his Whiggish eyes and begin to think that there might be something to this isolated maniacal dandy after all. He became my friend one morning after telling me that he 'quite liked' the book, and so he has remained, my faithful friend ever since, and the one man of my own rank whom I expect always to remain so. The rest of England's aristocracy will no doubt send only their carriages to my funeral. I expect Cam to come. And to say no more than he means.

Then there was Charles Skinner Matthews, with his mop of freethinking wild black hair, and his tight trousers that would never reach properly to his shoes no matter what his tailor did. Matthews, who used to call a *Miscellany*, which Hobhouse had published, and which failed to 'go off' satisfactorily, his *Miss-sell-any*, was always looked up to by me and the rest as by far the most amusing member of our circle. Unfortunately he was of a flippantly sceptical turn of mind, as brilliant pathics often are, and had no great delicacy about airing his republican opinions to all and sundry, but I am not aware that he had any other serious faults. In those days at Cambridge he used sometimes to join in the swimming exercises, but I always told him that he would be drowned if ever he came to a difficult pass in the water, as he swam too high out of it. In this I am much afraid that I knew what I was talking about, as shall be seen.

Other good friends of mine were William Bankes, the explorer, with his champagne-bottle shoulders, and the corpse-like Scrope Davies, a Fellow at King's and another rival swimmer, considered by some a not too desirable companion of mine in later days in London. Scrope was a gambler. He had one other passion which he satisfied by going once a month to a house of prostitution, always announcing his coming with a note reading thus: 'Dear Peggy, I shall be with you tomorrow evening between 8 and 9 o'clock. Whip and knout! Kindest regards....' He spoke with a stammer, made fun of my satanic ambitions, and called me 'the Old English Baron' because he said I was always going on about my family being one of the oldest English baronies, not some johnny-come-lately lordlings. We were all fine fellows, and belched and farted together, and spouted Homer, and munched marrons, and read French novels.

I kept a tame bear at Cambridge, in a turret at the

top of my staircase, which bear I used to say I intended to make sit for a fellowship, a not especially clever jibe, of which I was proud at the time. The name of that bear was Ursus Major. I kept it since of course dogs were forbidden.

For the rest, my university career was not remarkable. It provided, though, my first bite of freedom and taste of independence, and I set myself to enjoy it not wisely but too well. Yet, however it might be said to have been marred, particularly towards the end, by loose living – (and I then took an intense and insane pleasure in describing my life as a whirlwind of vice, and spoke of my conscience as a dead body devoured by corruption) – I must now confess without any dissimulation that I was never really a rampant lecher or inordinate drinker, and had, in fact, already at that time begun my almost continuous battle against a natural tendency to put on flesh. Though vanity has always been one of my motives in this, there is perhaps something not morally despicable in a long and weary struggle to 'keep fit' on the part of a man who is by no means indifferent to the allurements of appetite, though I have only a penny palate. After all, and even allowing for whatever rôle vanity must have played in this item of my life, it is certain that the chief inducement has been the necessity of keeping down my weight if my defective foot is to be of any practical use to me at all. For nearly the whole of my adult existence my main diet has consisted of dry biscuits and soda water. At times I have been almost mad with hunger and then I have occasionally indulged in an orgy of potatoes and fish mashed up together and drenched with vinegar, which I devour like a famished dog. And then (too often) I have had to pay for this indulgence by an attack of indigestion which causes me to roll on the floor in agony. Self-indulgent in general my life may have been, but I think no one can fairly deny that it has contained also an element of unusual self-control, and this habitual abstemiousness of mine may be regarded as all of a piece with a certain obstinate courage which has inspired and enabled me to take quite a large share in strenuous athletic pursuits, despite my physical handicap and despite the pain involved. Not that the vanity should be glossed over in a book whose one object is to try to represent or enact me *as I am*. And here is perhaps the place to confess that a friend while describing me as witty and agreeable, said that I am disgracefully conceited at bottom, thinking that everyone ought always to be talking about and admiring my poetry and myself. I do not know that this is true, but one cannot altogether ignore the impressions of one's friends; they may perhaps be truer than the face one sees in one's own private mirror.

Not that what one's friends perceive is always right. A tiny incident comes here to mind.... I recollect Scrope Davies coming suddenly into my bedroom (I think in 1807 when I was having my dandy fling) and finding me with my hair done up in curl-papers. 'Why, Byron,' says he, with that little viperish grin of his, 'I thought that your hair curled naturally!' 'So it does,' I replied. 'Every night!' Yet the fact is that in this instance (as in many others) I sacrificed the truth for a witticism. My hair *does* curl with some naturalness. The papers were merely an attempt to assist and hasten nature.

More worthy enthusiasms of my Cambridge days

were boxing and fencing, as well as some pistol-shooting. John ('Gentleman') Jackson, the champion pugilist of the time, was my corporeal pastor and master, and his picture still adorns the walls of my dressing room. It shows a truly formidable figure, though the face hardly comes up to expectations among the ladies. But then that profession is hardly one calculated to enhance beauty of countenance. Of equal repute was my fencing instructor, Henry Angelo, who shared rooms with Jackson at number 13 Bond Street. My happiest memories of university are of hours spent at my study with gloves or foils, though I can recollect also with pleasure the smell of a certain coffee-house in Benet Street where I liked to sit reading Pope and eating plum tarts on the sly. I was always a Papist in the verse I most admire; that little Queen Anne's man puts us all down.

Notwithstanding an allowance (£500 a year) which might have proved sufficient for a careful cove, I came down from Cambridge woefully in debt. My unhappy mother's anxiety was acute. I owed, I think, about nine or ten thousand pounds, and poor 'Spooney' (Hanson, our family lawyer) was almost badgered to death by creditors on the one hand and by me on the other. The fact is that I was never accustomed to deny myself anything save in the matter of food, and even then there was always the secret vice of the plum tarts to go with the poetry. It was a disgruntled sort of graduate who in 1808 bade farewell to the University which had thought as little of him as he had of it.

I parted again with Shelley on rather better terms tonight, even though he saw fit to observe in parting that he thought my present career must end soon in some violent circumstance. Earlier, we rode together on the Lido, coming back in my gondola past the island where the lunatics are kept. As we passed the island the bell in the church-tower was calling the prisoners to prayer. Shelley professed himself appalled as usual by anyone praying, and even more so lunatics. But I said that lunatics are perhaps in more need of praying than the rest of us. My friend's spirits remained subdued, and Margarita did not improve matters by *growling* when I tried to introduce him to her.

CHAPTER SEVEN

My Dog Goes Mad and Dies, While I Take my Seat in the House of Lords

It's raining. Allegra has gone to the Hoppners. I miss her nonsense. I have a toothache. The clock's stopped. One of the monkeys has been sick on the staircase and the smell is disgusting. Fletcher's out whoring. Besides all which, I confess I am already beginning to tire of this Margarita. My tiger mistress used to make me laugh, not least by her habit of stopping to cross herself if a church-bell rings anywhere in the distance while we are having sex. But now even this agreeably pagan practice has begun to pall. (There are altogether too many church-bells in Venice, and they ring indiscriminately day and night.) In her *fazziolo* Margarita looks beautiful, but alas! she longs for a hat and feathers, like some little Brighton gold-digger, and as fast as I throw her hats into the fire, she buys more with my money. Also, she is damnably jealous of my other loves, and her behaviour grows more and more ungovernable as her confidence in my company increases. On the last night of the Carnival, she snatched the mask from the face of Madame Contarini, who was on my arm. I reproached her, saying that she shouldn't do this to a lady of high birth, '*una dama*', and so forth.

She answered, *'Se ella è dama, mi io son Veneziana'* ('She may be a lady, but I am a Venetian.') This would have been fine five hundred years ago. But, alas! Venice, and her people, and her nobles, are alike returning fast to the ocean.

Quite *how* I am going to get rid of Margarita is another matter, and one not to be resolved tonight. . . .

Reader, I confess that at the point which I have reached in the story of my days I gave serious thought to the possibility of selling my soul – that is to say, Newstead Abbey. It would have been a sure way out of my pecuniary embarrassments, after all. However, a few months spent living in the place soon convinced me that Newstead was not (at that time) for selling. It was like living in the intellectual and emotional landscape of one of my own early poems: the moss-encrusted walls, the melancholy ivy, the roses with the worms in them, the rot. Also the vistas of wind and rain and hopeless grandeur. Not to speak of the hundred mournful noises which were the immediate music of the house: creaks and sighs, the groaning of timber and the dripping of water. Come what may, I decided, Newstead and I must for the time being stand or fall together. Having lived on the spot, having fixed my restless heart upon it, I persuaded myself without trouble (but with considerable self-deception, as will be seen) that no pressure, past or future, no ghost or money-lender, curse or dun, would ever induce me to barter this last essential vestige of my inheritance. I had that pride within me at the time which enables a man to support difficulties and believe himself a hero because of them. I endured privations there, and afflictions worse than Lord Grey de Ruthyn's phallus at my fundament, but could I have obtained for Newstead Abbey the finest fortune in the country I believe I would have rejected the proposition out of hand. Spooney was forever urging me to sell to pay my debts and secure my future. I felt like a man of honour in those days and I was utterly and magnificently determined that I would not sell my home.

In this resolve I may say that I believe myself to have been as sincere as in any other. Yet I must hasten to insult myself by adding that in 1812 things seemed to me sufficiently otherwise to enable me to profit by some £25,000 paid as a forfeit by a Mr Claughton who had agreed to purchase my property for £140,000 but then failed to complete the contract. And now, this very year, the whole estate is in the process of being finally sold to an old schoolfellow of mine, Thomas Wildman, now a Colonel in the army. Things are different now, after all, changed utterly. I shall never set foot in England again.

Still, in my hot youth I took this innocent and affectionate pride in the damp-sodden seat of my ancestors, where, in part at least, I busied myself living the simple life, and spent much of my time on *English Bards* and a fistful of lyrics. It was my chief pleasure, as I remember it, to lie on my back among the cushions in the bottom of a boat on the lake, looking up at the blueness of the summer sky and thinking of nothing in particular though no doubt if asked I would have said that I brooded on Fate or Destiny or somesuch high-falutin toothache. I liked to read in this boated situation also. When tired of reading or daydreaming thus, and perhaps a little sticky from my exertions, I would just roll over into the cold comfort of the waters of the lake, to be promptly rescued by my beloved Newfoundland dog, Boatswain.

Boatswain was a good dog, loyal and affectionate, but alas he caught the rabies, and died in a fit of madness even as I wiped the froth from his mouth with my bare hand. He has this to his credit above several women I have known: even when he went crazy, he bit nobody but himself. The loss was a great grief to me, and I had a tomb erected on the site of the altar in the ruined chapel of the Abbey, with the following words inscribed on one side of the pedestal supporting an antique urn:

Near this spot
Are deposited the remains of one
Who possessed Beauty without Vanity
Strength without Insolence
Courage without Ferocity
And all the Virtues of Man without his Vices.
This praise which would be unmeaning Flattery
If inscribed over human ashes
Is but a just tribute to the Memory of
BOATSWAIN, a Dog
Who was born at Newfoundland, May 1803,
And died at Newstead Abbey, November 18, 1808.

I may say that it is my wish and intent to keep Boatswain company there when my own time comes. I offered the same facility once to my manservant Joe Murray, that ancient gentleman I inherited from my uncle along with the amputated forest and the Abbey itself. Old Joe, though, failed to appreciate the honour. 'My lord may lie with dogs if he pleases,' said he, 'but I would rather be buried like a Christian.'

Newstead delighted me in many ways, not least for the variety of its apartments. My bedroom there, for instance, was known as the Rook Cell, from its proximity to the colony of those birds that cawed all the time among the old oaks outside its window. It was reached by a winding stone stair, like that of a church tower, and from it a door opened into another (smaller) chamber known as the haunted room because a Black Brother is supposed to appear there before a death in the house or a change in the ownership of the Abbey. This room was the one in which sick or dying monks used to be placed in order that they might hear the offices in the chapel, which that particular corner of the building adjoins. I found it the perfect ante-chamber to a sleeping apartment.

There was also at Newstead a dungeon which I delighted to use as a bath. It was a kind of cellar situated at the side of one of the old cloisters, entered by steep stone steps, and very dark. This cheerful swimming-bath of mine was formerly the mortuary where the bodies of the monks lay before burial. Speaking of the monks, I had also at this time a drinking-cup fashioned from the skull of one of these fine fellows. It had been dug up in the grounds, the skull, and I had it mounted in silver and made available for convivial purposes, a juvenile decadence which I now consider reprehensible in that its style is *borrowed* and from impure sources (Beckford, Monk Lewis, and so forth). I did not drink from this skull, however, on Sunday the 22nd of January, 1809, which was the day I came of age. All the same, there were celebrations of a sort at Newstead, things consonant with the pressure of its master's poverty, a small ox being roasted for my tenants and dependants. But I myself was absent in London, installed at Reddish's Hotel in St James's Street, and marked the occasion by dining on eggs and bacon and a bottle of ale. These are my favourite dish and drinkable, in fact, but as neither the eggs and bacon nor the ale agree with me I never use them but on great jubilees and junkets – once in five years or so.

On the 13th of March of this same year I took my seat in the House of Lords, and was sore offended with my cousin and guardian, Lord Carlisle, for the coldness and the sour long face with which he saw fit to greet my implied request for advice and assistance in this rather formidable ordeal. I had asked for his support and protection in order to be duly presented in the assembly. He responded with a culpable indifference, mislaying the necessary legal documents also in order to retard my reception, and refusing to introduce me to my peers. For my part, I fear that I perhaps offended in my turn the Lord Chancellor, Eldon, by the lack of warmth with which I received his greeting. In this incident he mistook my public seriousness for private disdain. My coldness was the studied air of one who feared that a more cordial manner might be interpreted as an inclination of readiness to join a party. I wished to have nothing to do with any party.

Always excepting house-parties, that is. Less than a month after taking my seat in the Lords, I returned to Newstead to entertain a little group of bachelor intimates, among whom were Hobhouse, Matthews, Scrope Davies, and some others – seven or eight of us in all. We amused ourselves fairly idiotically by dressing up as monks and indulging in the revels described with quite imposing exaggeration at the beginning of *Childe Harold's Pilgrimage*. The proceedings, truth to tell, were actually on a more modest scale than my poem implies, the 'Paphian Girls' of my fiction being in reality two skinny housemaids and a certain married woman deficient in shame, who had once when riding with me at Brighton dressed herself as a boy so as to pass as my brother. Alas, she was lacking a little in the verbal dexterity such a sibling relation might have been expected to put forward. Having her mount admired by an elderly lady acquaintance of mine, this person lamentably betrayed the lie we were enacting by the fluent response, 'Yus, the 'oss was *gave* me by me bruvver!'

Our house-party at Newstead kept late hours, rising at one (with the exception of Citizen Matthews, who gained for himself a unique reputation by turning out at eleven) and never finishing breakfast before half-past two. We would then pass the rest of the day in riding, boxing, fencing, boating, and swimming in the lake, practising with pistols, and playing with the bear and the wolf which I kept chained beside the front door. As their host, I was known to them all as the Abbot, a name which has stuck to me among these particular friends in subsequent years, despite (or perhaps because of) my markedly unmonastic rule of life. Still, reports of our wildness at that house-party and others have been foolishly embellished and vulgarised by those anxious to discredit me as a mere seeker after sensations. In truth most of our pleasures were innocent to the point of puerility, though they caused us much laughter as is common when young men so indulge themselves together. For instance, one night Hobhouse in passing down the Long Gallery heard this hollow groan issuing from a stone coffin which had been unearthed by me in a vain search for treasure which I half-believed to be buried beneath the cloisters. As he approached to investigate, trembling just a whit more than suited a professed sceptic, up rose from the coffin a figure in monkish garb which blew out his candle with a single breath! Hobhouse might have fainted or turned Papist on the spot, had not a wicked high-pitched giggle in the dark revealed to him that his assailant was nothing more ghostly than Citizen Matthews.

Still, you might say that all this comprised a distinctly silly set of doings on which to base the opening stanzas of one of the less ridiculous long poems in the English language – and you would be right. I mention our penchant for trivialities merely to contradict the report of the fiery and licentious life which some have assumed was mine in those days at the Abbey. I brought no paramours there with me from London; I seduced few serving-maids. A lot of my time at Newstead was passed supine on the sofa, reading. Lying on my back and turning the pages of a book at regular intervals has always been one of my favourite forms of physical pleasure. To be sure, with the young gentlemen of my acquaintance I played a number of mad pranks, yet nothing was done but what young gentlemen may do without harm to themselves or others. As for the times, more plentiful than not, when there was no company present at Newstead either to amuse me or to be amused, and I was not to be found reading *The Dunciad* on my sofa nor adrift in my boat on the lake, then I would very likely be immersing myself for hours in a hot bath or trotting up and down the hills in the park, my body all wrapped and loaded with seven waistcoats and a heavy topcoat and scarves. These strange physical activities derived from nothing more sinister or wholesome than my war to keep down my weight, a war which I have waged to the present day, with most battles won. When I was nineteen years old, I weighed 14 stones and 6 pounds. By the time of my twentieth birthday, I had got this down to 10 stones and 7 pounds. I have never risen grossly above the lower level since, though this has meant that I have gone through much of my life hungry. It is nothing for me to fast for 48 hours. Just two years ago I was living on a constant diet of one thin slice of bread for breakfast, a dinner of raw vegetables, and only green tea and soda water in between. Nowadays when it occurs to me that I am starving, I chew tobacco, mastic gum, or laudanum. What a contrast, to be sure, with the picture of Lord Byron which all the young ladies of London believe in. But then discordance is my favourite mode, in life as in literature. I was always the man who spills a dish of tea over his testicles in handing a cup to his charmer, to the great shame of his nankeen breeches.

CHAPTER EIGHT

I Proceed on my First Pilgrimage, and Swim the Hellespont, and Save a Girl in a Sack

Sir, – With great grief I inform you of the death of my late dear Master, my Lord, who died this morning at ten of the clock of a rapid decline and slow fever, caused by anxiety, sea-bathing, women, and riding in the sun against my advice....

Sent a letter off thus, to Hobhouse, this morning, signing it 'Fletcher'. But the joke is really on me. For the first time in my life, I suppose it is physically possible that I should die of women, or rather of one woman, the Margarita animal. In my early innocence, I considered her a bird of passage. Now, though, she exhibits all the usual abysmal signs of nest-making, slapping my other women, frightening my valet with her ferocious house-keeping and even Tita my gondolier with her passionate knife-sharpening, feeding too many bonbons to the monkeys and the fox, filling the whole household with terror and indigestion. I cannot have it much longer. One of us will have to go, and since I am paying the yearly rental (4800 francs) on this place, it had better be her.

Comforting myself as is my wont with a little authorship, I come to the time when in order to escape somewhat from myself I went on my first pilgrimage.

To leave England was an absolute necessity of my mental life. Passing from the fogs of home, I felt as if I was bursting the bars of a prison in which I had spent all my days. For a splendid interlude, I experienced a delight heretofore unknown to me; my morbid ideals, my melancholy, my doubts and my despair, all fell into the bosom of the warm blue waters of the South, as if the amorous kisses of the sea-breeze penetrated into my soul. Nothing, I think, invigorates and assuages me so much as the grand spectacles of Nature – the wind, caught and taught by the swelling canvas; the foamy waves, rent and furrowed by a conquering keel; a dark depth of fathoms beneath my feet, and an infinite height of brightness above my head; life on all sides, wheeling, whirling, intoxicating me with its voluptuousness; the salt-sweet smell of marine vegetation mingling with my blood; the vigour of man's unconquerable will manifested by his struggle with the elements, and the human dignity realised at each moment by each small victory. My soul invariably grows a little younger when I have to travel on the ocean. All the same, that is quite enough general marine philosophy for one chapter. Nor do I propose now to provide any detailed incidental account of my two years' absence from England, from the July of 1809 to the same month of 1811. The jaunt had some lasting influence both on my career and my fame, but for its essential spirit I suppose the reader had better consult the poem which had its issue from this journey – I mean, of course, *Childe Harold's Pilgrimage*. There I said just about all that I have to say on the subject of my early life represented as a voyage of self-discovery, with as many meditations as anyone ever needed upon the wreckage of empires, Greek freedom, mountains, Time, destiny, the sea, and what have you. It is my intent to mention here only such particular things as bear out the purpose of the present work by casting light or dark upon my character.

I remember, on board the packet, keeping myself aloof from the other passengers, in best Childe Harold-like manner, leaning against the rail and shrouds in the tranquillity of the moonlight. It was my wish to seem almost apparitional. To this end, I spent only one evening in the cabin with the rest of them. Among these other passengers was John Galt, the Scotch novelist, but I confess that I was not at the time in a mood to do justice to Mr Galt. His mildness and equanimity did strike me, but, to say the truth, his manner had not deference enough for my then aristocratic tastes, and finding I could not awe him into a respect sufficiently profound for my sublime self, either as a peer or as a poet, I felt a little rankling grudge towards him. That has now worn off. I believe that Galt suspected me of pride and irascibility, in which he would not have been far wrong. In those days, as I have admitted, my aristocracy was very fierce. It has been considerably modified as I have become perhaps a more mature man of the world. Yet I believe I have always been prepared for my part to recognise the claims of real worth or ability in whatever rank they might be found.

What do I now recall of all my journeys? Passing through the storm-tossed Bay of Biscay, of course, and being sick in my hat; and then the enchanted and enchanting shores of ancient Lusitania, the wide mouth of the Tagus, and all around about the mountains with their lofty peaks half-veiled in clouds, the golden fruits hidden under broad emerald leaves, the air filled with such aromas that I could hardly breathe for excitement. In my mind's eye I may still see Lisbon beholding herself in the mirror of her bright waters, and the blooming groves of Cintra, through whose narrow streets one can just perceive a monastery inhabited by penitents, and the crosses which mark the scenes of murders and assassinations. Above all, I remember always the granite rocks with their dentated summits, which seemed – in the quick changes from light to darkness – to be moved by the wind. Then those deep dark valleys, where the northern vegetation mourns the absence of the sun, their declivities covered with orange-trees, their heights crowned with silver honeysuckle, the roar of a thousand streams breaking into cascades, and the distant prospect of the ocean reflecting the light on her azure bosom. I saw a bull-fight in Cadiz and fell in love with a Mrs Constance Spencer-Smith in Malta. The bull took more finishing off than the lady.

As a poet I desired above all to visit the land of original artistic forms, the realm of their perfect expression: I mean, Greece. There is no country in the world that has so completely carried out and embodied the beauty of ideas as Greece. From my vessel there, coasting among the Greek promontories, I saw the shadow of that rock which overhangs the sea of Leucades, where Sappho appeased in the waters the infinite desires of her heart. From thence also I beheld the little bay in which the practical genius of the West, personified by Augustus, overcame the more exalted genius of the East, represented by that powerful but luxurious Mark Antony, he who sacrificed his love for Rome to his devotion to Cleopatra, the maga, poetess, enchantress, cat-goddess, capable of reviving with her soft embraces and hard dances the Oriental theogony even in the Grecian temples. I saw Mount Parnassus covered with snow, and I inscribed my name like any other vandal on the temple at Sounion.

After passing by the shores of Attica, I progressed to Albania, where I was much attracted by a spectacle quite opposed to Hellenic severity: by the Oriental customs, the hyperbole, the sensual habits, and the voluptuous feasts of Asia. I suffered one gonorrhea, two attacks of Tertian fever, and some haemorrhoides.

I had done some small shooting at Southwell, rather because it was the thing to do than from any country love of it. (What I would have adored to shoot was of course Lord Grey de Ruthyn.) I disliked field sports even when I took a very minor part in them, and was always fond of animals, especially dogs. Of course, it is by killing that we join in their fun, but it was during the course of this first pilgrimage that I shot my last bird. This was an eaglet which I fired at on the shores of the Gulf of Lepanto, near Vostitza. The creature was only wounded, and I tried to save it, the eye was so bright. But it pined and died in a few days, gazing at the sky, and I never did since, and never will, attempt the death of another bird.

If that young eagle's eye distressed me most, nothing flattered me more during the whole tour than my interview at Tepelene with Ali Pasha. In a white-marble pavilion, from the centre of which rose a murmuring fountain, reclining on soft cushions of richest silk, on one side an amber dish of perfume, and coffee on the other, before each of us a long pipe, with golden light streaming through the lattice and half revealing the palms that mingled with the cypresses – in such a scene we conversed, Ali Pasha and I, surrounded by Albanians in their tasselled caps, and Macedonians in their red mantles, and negroes brought at great cost from Nubia. He told me, Ali Pasha, that he was sure that I was a man of birth because I had small ears, curling hair, and little white hands. For years I was delighted with this description, God knows why. Nowadays I am inclined to vote it more appropriate to a barber's assistant. Ali Pasha also told me that he was very partial to Englishmen, particularly English sailors. He invited me to visit him at night, an invitation that I ducked with difficulty.

Off Corfu, in a Turkish ship of war, owing to the ignorance of the captain and crew, I was nearly lost, though the storm was not so very violent. Night came worse than the day had been, and a sudden shift of wind, about midnight, threw the vessel into a trough of the sea, which struck her aft, tore away the rudder, started the stem-post, and shattered the whole of her stern-frame. Fletcher yelled after his wife (who was at Newstead), the Greeks called on all the saints, the Mussulmans on Allah; the captain burst into tears and ran below deck, instructing us to pray to God. Hobhouse – I forgot to mention that my friend Cam was my companion on this Grand Tour – believed that I behaved on this occasion with a coolness and courage which he found admirable. In truth, discovering that my lameness prevented me from being of any real use in the emergency, I wrapt myself up in my travelling-cloak and lay down on the deck where I went to sleep. Whether this was from courage or weariness combined with acceptance of the facts and a reluctance to pray, I leave for others to judge. Among my faults, *lack* of courage has never had a place, I think I may say that.

So I should mention also my swim, with which I am still quite pleased, across the Hellespont from Sestos to Abydos, in the wake of Leander. I was not particularly concerned to show whether Leander had been a decent swimmer, nor whether poets lie. I take it that the wiser part of mankind already knows that poets lie, and the matter is not of much interest, and certainly never required my disproof by getting wet but not drowned in the Hellespont. I was inspired to my swim by a wish to do the thing for myself, that is all. This has been sufficient inspiration, truth to tell, for a good nine tenths of my life's adventures. Anyway, in my swimming the Hellespont I was accompanied by a Mr William Ekenhead, an officer of the frigate *Salsette.* It was a cold swim of over four miles, in a tricky transverse current, and it took me an hour and ten minutes. I was never lame in water. There is in fact a mermaid in my family crest, supporting the motto *Crede Byron.* And here in Venice there are those who sometimes call me 'the English fish'.

My 'Maid of Athens' belongs also to this tour. Her real name was Teresa Macri and she was the youngest of three sisters, all of them under fifteen years of age, with whose widowed mother I lived for a time in the Greek capital. This girl was the divinity in whose service I adopted the uncomfortable local custom of inflicting upon myself a wound across the breast in token of my devotion. At least, I think she was. I have still a distinct recollection of a pair of ice-cold blue eyes looking on during the painful operation, plainly considering it nothing more than a fit tribute to their owner's beauty, but by no means moved to tears of gratitude. If those eyes did not sit in the sockets of Teresa Macri then it may have been one of her sisters who owned them, Mariana or Kattinka, or at any rate a similar Hellenic charmer from just down the street, or round the corner, or in that quarter. The Maid of Athens of my verse fiction is now more real to me than Teresa Macri or her sisters. Is this so terrible? Reality is only paper thin itself, and perhaps the Muse may sometimes be more real than the mortal creatures in whom she takes up her residence from time to time in order to delight and appall us. I remember the pleasure and the pang of cutting my flesh with that sharp little knife in honour of the youthful cold blue eyes that watched me do so. I may now refer to my poem about the Maid of Athens. That is over there on a certain page in a blue-bound book. The rest is a blur of biography, and not especially interesting. In any case, I remember Teresa's mother eventually tried to sell her daughter to me for £600, which rather spolit Teresa as a Muse embodiment.

At Athens at this time I contracted also a sort of passing acquaintance with the traveller and adventurer Lady Hester Stanhope. Her age and her well-celebrated homeliness imposed obstacles to love, but the exaltation of her character and the poetical tendency of her disposition united us in the strictest relations of spiritual brother-and-sister-hood. Lady Hester had herself fled from the fogs of England in search of Eastern light and beauty, and on entering these Asiatic regions she had laid aside her Protestant creed as the serpent casts its skin. When I met her, her Bible was the universe; her Deity, the unimaginable Infinite; and her profession, prophecy, as in the times of the Sibyls. Her only motive in existence, as I understand it, was a certain restless poetry, incapable of expression, which, being unable to embody itself in words or works, excited her to wild actions and a wandering life. But her leading characteristic, it must be said, was a real (although sublime) mental derangement. This gifted and virile woman would have passed for a miracle of prevision and prophetic power if her death had not disclosed her insanity. However, I fear that I made a less than favourable impression upon her. I believe that she reported that I was at one time mopish, and nobody was to speak to me, while another time I was for being jocular with everybody. Then she said that I was a sort of Don Quixote, fighting with the police for a woman of the town, and then that I wanted to make myself something great. I know she thought that I had a dark deal of vice in my looks, my eyes being set too close together for her approval, and my brow being too contracted. A mutual female acquaintance of the two of us once repeated to me that Lady Hester had said to her that the only good thing about my looks was this part – drawing her hand under her cheek and down the front of her neck. And the curl on my forehead, she conceded. I mention all this nonsense because how others see us is of interest, or ought to be. I suspect that Lady Hester Stanhope disliked what she took to be my politics (which is really my whole cast of mind) rather more than she cared one way or the other about my physiognomy. I was at that time some sub-species of Whig. I have since then simplified my political position into an utter detestation of all existing governments. God will not always be a Tory.

This fighting with the police like Don Quixote, by the way, probably refers to an incident which took place late in 1810, after Hobhouse had left me and returned home to England. One evening as I rode on horseback through the Piraeus, I saw a group of Turks dragging along a large sack. I had a presentiment as to what that sack contained when I observed that it was wriggling, and so interfered with the procession with, I may say, a certain determination, threatening the leader of the party with a loaded pistol. The sack was opened, and I beheld a young girl, pale as a corpse, but beautiful. Her crime, so it seemed, was Mary Magdalene's one of too much loving, and her punishment was that she was about to be thrown in this sack into the Aegean. I remember remarking that if every promiscuous woman in England were thrown into the sea, they would pave a causeway so that a man might walk from Dover to Calais. Well, by a mixture of bribery, entreaty, and threats I managed to get the girl reprieved, a condition of her reprieve being that she left Athens. (You will find a considerable transmogrification of these simple events in my poem *The Giaour*.) Such things, incidentally, were by no means uncommon. That same Ali Pasha who so hospitably received me in his palace once caused twelve Turkish women accused of infidelity to be sewn up in sacks and thrown into the Bosphorus. Not one of them complained. They all accepted death with resignation and in silence – beautiful toys of destiny, broken like well-wrought glass against the rocks! Such beauties aside, I learned to dislike and despise the Turks and all they do, having seen dogs snarling over a human corpse left out in the street to rot at Constantinople.

At Patras, in that same autumn of 1810, I was prostrated by an attack of malarial fever and almost killed not by the fever but by my physicians. The chief of these assassins was named Romanelli. He was a surly fat quack in a bad blond wig who had waged a campaign for eighteen years against the sick of Otranto, killing many and wounding the rest. (The other doctor who attended me was merely a fool who trusted his own implicit genius, never having studied medicine.) In three days of leeches and potions, this villain Romanelli brought me to what I fondly supposed was my last gasp, and in this condition I penned my own epitaph. It is vile verse, but not bad for a dying man:

Youth, Nature, and relenting Jove
To keep my lamp IN strongly strove;
But Romanelli was so stout
He beat all three – and blew it OUT!

The reason why I am not presently lying at peace under a slab of marble with these words above me is that my two Albanian servants of the time rescued me by declaring that they would cut Dr Romanelli's throat if a speedy cure were not effected. With the result that Dr Romanelli never called again, and I recovered.

With regard to the unsociable habits of which Mr Galt and Lady Hester Stanhope saw fit to complain, I should say that while I can be convivial and even entertaining enough on the odd occasion, a love of solitude has always been integral to my nature. As I wrote towards the end of Harold's pilgriming:

Oh! that the Desert were my dwelling-place,
With one fair Spirit for my minister,
That I might all forget the human race,
And, hating no one, love but only her!

Though I might find that actual condition a little too much of a good thing, still to be alone to a considerable extent is essential to me, the no less so because it has been largely my chosen mode of life right from the beginning. The hours spent lying on that tomb in Harrow churchyard are just one glimpse of this. I must confess that I have never passed two hours in any company without wishing myself out of it. Friendly though I was with Hobhouse, for instance, his departure homeward half-way through our travels came as a relief. He stayed with me, after all, for a whole year, and in my view twelve months of any given individual is perfect ipecacuanha. As for women – alas, we cannot live with them any more than we can live without them. I am in any case forbade the company of the one fair Spirit I would want above all others. But I will come to that in due course, when I have to.

My enjoyment of my two years' peregrination – more especially the second part of it – was marred by a cause too sordid to be introduced into the idealised version of it given in *Childe Harold*: worry about ways and means. In vain I wrote to my mother and to Spooney begging them to send me supplies; neither of them could satisfy my necessities. My pilgrimage had been undertaken upon borrowed money, partly by means of a life insurance, and more than once it seemed likely to come to a premature and ignominious end. Now, as the time to return approached, I was faced by the uncongenial prospect of much business to be done with lawyers and creditors. This, to a man who hates bustle as he hates a bishop, was a serious concern. All I brought home from my travels were some pieces of marble, some Greek skulls found in ancient sepulchres, three servants, two tortoises, and a phial containing juice from the plant which poisoned Socrates.

Addendum: Unable to sleep, I just read this over (not at all my usual practice, I might say). It occurs to me to add that as well as the poison &c, I brought back *Childe Harold*, begun on 31 October 1809, at Jannina, a few days after meeting Ali Pasha; completed in Smyrna by the end of March the next year; revised and slightly enlarged early in 1811 at Athens. The stanza for my poem I took of course from Spenser's *Faerie Queene*, extracts from which I had with me in an anthology. However, as I will make clear in my next chapter, at that time I had no very high opinion of my achievement in this work (originally called *Childe Burun*, which tells all).

The other thing I should add is that apart from the life insurance, Harold/Burun/I went on this pilgrimage thanks largely to the kindness of our good friend Scrope. He lent me the money for it out of his winnings from one single night's glorious gaming in Almack's. I found him in his lodgings, dead drunk, beside a chamber pot brimming with banknotes, and on his lapel this note: 'Take what you want, Byron, but don't wake me up.'

Dear Scrope! He was uncommonly generous to me; uncommonly patient, as well, in waiting for his money back.

By the by, while on my travels I heard somewhere of an ancient Latin text (anonymous, of course) called *The History of Nemo*. In this book Nemo or 'nobody' is to be interpreted as a *name*. Thus, everything impossible, inadmissible, or forbidden, is, on the contrary, permitted to our friend Nemo. And thanks to this transposition, friend Nemo acquires the peculiar aspect of being equal almost to God – (or at least, the Devil) – endowed with unique, exceptional powers and knowledge (because he knows after all that which no one else knows) and extraordinary freedom (since he is allowed to do everything which nobody is permitted to do). Tonight I am Nemo. Every poet sometimes is. But I am the one and only *Lord* Nemo. Nothing, my lord. But old Lear had it right. Nothing will come of nothing. So good-night.

CHAPTER NINE

MY MOTHER DIES; I AWAKE ONE MORNING AND FIND MYSELF FAMOUS

I HAVE BEGUN A new poem, to be called *Don Juan*, and already completed a canto of it. It is intended to be a little quietly facetious upon everything. It is also epic, and burlesque, and when finished will have twelve books, a gale at sea (just like *The Odyssey*), a list of ships (just like *The Iliad*), and a general theme of love and war with many episodes of travel and tempest (as in Homer, Virgil, and the better shafts of Shakespeare). Yet I have no plan for my poem, only materials. As to my method, it is thoroughly *modern* in that it favours digression and improvisation, perpetually and briskly shifting in mood and tone, providing an impatient effect which I trust may amount to an utter discontinuity of thoughts and feelings. My stanza is the classical Italian octave, but absolutely Anglicised and debunked as in Frere's *Whistlecraft*. As for Donny Johnny himself, it is not my ambition to compete with Amadeus Mozart, merely to employ the dago as a peg for my digressions. Here is a stanza which I just wrote on the back of the last page of this first canto. I had hoped to fit it in somewhere, but see now that it will serve better perhaps as a sort of epigraph to my experiment with these *Memoirs*:

I would to Heaven that I were so much clay,
As I am blood, bone, marrow, passion, feeling –
Because at least the past were passed away,
And for the future – (but I write this reeling,
Having got drunk exceedingly to-day,
So that I seem to stand upon the ceiling)
I say – the future is a serious matter –
And so – for God's sake – hock and soda-water!

Not that I am actually drunk, or anyone ever wrote three lines worth the reading in any chemically or alchemically improved condition (with the possible exception of Coleridge and his *Kubla Khan*). To *read* as though I were drunk – that is the thing; to intoxicate the reader with my spirits, high and low.

Margarita just stalked in half-undressed to wish me goodnight. This she did with a Venetian benediction: '*Benedetto te, e la terra che ti fara!*' – 'May you be blessed, and the *earth* which you will *make*.' Is that not pretty? She can still occasionally please me with such expressions. A month ago I would have taken ten minutes out from my labours with my pen to belabour her a little with my penis. Now I merely record her wistful passage through my chamber, and pass back quickly to the story of my days.

Two years of childish pilgrimage at an end, I returned to England in the long wet summer of 1811, to be welcomed with something like delight by the earnest and ever-loyal Hobhouse, temporarily adopting the monstrous disguise of a soldier. Another friend also now plays a not unimportant part in the history of my fame. This is Robert Dallas, a novelist and my kinsman, who had first claimed acquaintance with me on the publication of *Hours of Idleness*. His deferential appreciation of what he was pleased to consider my genius was gratifying. Dallas was a decent creature, tall, willowy, with a face that looked as if it had been left in the bath too long, a fellow rather given over to moralizing, but sound. He set himself the penance or vocation of winning me, his young relative, into better ways. In this he failed, but the exercise was orthodox and no doubt did no harm to his own immortal part. I confess that I enjoyed shocking Dallas and bamboozling him. It took me quite some months to tire of all his efforts at reclamation. Dear old Dallas was a true friend, and it is a pleasure to salute him as being the first to recognise whatever merit there may be in *Childe Harold's Pilgrimage*. That recognition came about in this way. . . .

When we dined together at Reddish's Hotel in St James's Street, he asked eagerly as to the poetic fruits of my two years abroad. Believing then, as I still do now, that satire was my true forte, I was pleased to tell him that I had written a poem called *Hints from Horace*, a paraphrase of the Latin farmer, somewhat in the style of *English Bards*. Dallas took this manuscript home to read. However, he was disappointed. We breakfasted together the next morning and, after it became apparent that he didn't much care for my *Hints*, he asked rather despairingly whether nothing else had been written, wondering at the fact that I had penned not a single line in direct response to what he considered ought to have been the stimulation of my travels in foreign parts.

Somewhat grudgingly, I confessed that I *had* scribbled a great many stanzas, in the Spenserian measure, relative to these wanderings. But I told him that I didn't think much of them. I pressed Dallas to do whatever he could to get the *Hints from Horace* out.

My friend promised to do what he could with the *Hints*, so I let him go off with this second bundle of manuscripts under his arm. But if Dallas had been disappointed before, he was ecstatic now. That same evening he wrote to me: 'You have written one of the most delightful poems I have ever read. I have been so fascinated by *Childe Harold* that I have not been able to lay it down.'

This was pleasant, but I was still unpersuaded. I thought my *Hints* superior, and once more sought to persuade Dallas so when next we met. However, I told my friend at the same time that he was welcome to the Spenserian stuff he liked so much, which so far as I am concerned amounts to just a series of meditations on places and events given a sort of spurious unity by the shadow that is Harold, which is to say myself on stilts. I had made up my mind at this stage, in any case, that it was *infra dig* for a peer of the realm to accept money for what he wrote, even immortal verse, and I made a vow that I would never do so – a vow which I have since wisely modified. It is satisfactory to note here that the decent Dallas benefitted by his part in these proceedings to the tune of £600. (The *Hints*, by the by, remain unpublished to this day, but will doubtless buy another dog his dinner when the popular literary taste reverts to the stronger sensible ways of Pope and Dryden, always my masters, rather than all this simple-minded drivel of 'natural' slackness brought in by Turdsworth and his Lakeland tadpoles.) Despite my reservations, I was anxious that if the wretched *Childe* must see the light then it should issue forth from a mother of some standing, so after one or two disconcerting near-miscarriages – it was refused by Miller, of Albemarle Street, on account of my attack on the noble marble-hunter Elgin, whose publisher Miller happened to be – I gave Dallas a free hand, whereupon he sent my poem to John Murray, of Fleet Street, whose father, an ex-officer of the Royal Marines, had founded a publishing firm in 1768. Thus began one of the less miserable misalliances of my life, for Murray has remained my publisher to this day.

All that pother, plus law business, detained me in London for about a fortnight, and prevented me from arriving at Newstead until just too late to find my mother alive. Her death in fact was violent as her own character. She was already suffering, when the local cabinet-maker and upholsterer together presented her with their bills for certain necessary refurbishments made to the house. My mamma fell into a passion which ended in a fit of apoplexy, and killed her like a thunderbolt. With what looks suspiciously like premonition, I heard that she had said to her maid Mrs Bye only three days before this event, 'If I should be dead when Byron comes down, what a strange thing it would be!' However, I admit I had this story from the maid, and on the maid's word only, and it is well known that maids are made of such stuff.

It is awful to me now to remember that just before my departure abroad in Harold's cloak, two years previous, my mother and I had had one of our most terrible scenes, involving the decapitation of a statue with a poker. Perhaps it is as well for me to confess that by the time of her death my feeling for her was little short of total aversion. It was to her own false delicacy at my birth that I owe my twisted foot, and yet, as far as I can remember back into my childhood, she never ceased to taunt and reproach me for being a cripple. Even a few days before we parted, she in one of her fits of passion uttered an imprecation upon me, praying that I might prove as ill-formed in mind as I am in body. (If she could read this first canto of *Don Juan*, I daresay she would consider it an answer to that mother's prayer.)

Bearing some of this in mind, perhaps it might yet be conceded that my general behaviour towards her was not utterly unfilial. I wrote to her constantly while I was away, as I believe good sons are supposed to do, and as I remember it my very last letter to her, written from London, expressed my regret that I was unable to return to her more quickly, and the hope that she would consider Newstead as her house and myself only as a visitor. On hearing of her sickness, which I did on 31st July, I hastened to the Abbey as fast as carriage would bear me, but the news of her death came to me while I was on the way. I brought back for her from my travels a shawl and some attar of roses. These gifts I placed within her coffin. Despite all our differences, sitting beside it I felt the truth of Mr Gray's observation, 'That we can have only one mother.' (Peace be with her! – which it will be, since I am not. . . .) Then, on the day of the funeral, I found that I could not follow the procession to the church of Hucknall Torkard. I stood in the door of the Abbey and watched the hearse depart. When it was out of sight, I called on young Robert Rushton, the son of a tenant, who was one of my man-servants, and told him to fetch the gloves for a spar. But I boxed without my usual enthusiasm, hitting too violently, and soon threw the gloves away.

The links of life's chain, once shaken, break easily. Just two days later I learned of the sudden death of my friend Charles Skinner Matthews, that staunch republican, Socratic sodomite, and sometime ghost. He had become entangled in a bed of weeds while bathing in the Cam, and drowned. I felt at the time that some curse was hanging over me and mine. My mother lay in the ground at Hucknall Torkard; one of my best friends was drowned in a ditch. Then, about a week afterwards, I heard also of the death of Edleston, the chorister at Cambridge whose voice had been music to me even when he did not sing. Perhaps this last sad death surprised me least. From the first time I saw him, I thought that John Edleston would prove but a passing apparition in this world, like a flower or a butterfly. (His very name, I just now noticed, doodling with its letters in the margin of my text, is itself an anagram of 'Lost Eden'.)

These three blows followed upon each other so rapidly that I was quite stupid from the shock, and though I ate and drank and talked and even laughed at times, yet for a while I could hardly persuade myself that I was awake. I invited Hobhouse to Newstead, and together we drank to Matthews' memory. When he had gone again, I busied myself with a little orgy of sensual comfort involving the girls on the estate. I played the disciplinarian, issuing an edict for the abolition of caps, saying no hair was to be cut on any pretext. Stays I permitted, but not too low before.

In November of that same year, a more cheerful experience befell me. Tom Moore, the Irish poet, had five years previously engaged in a serio-comic sort of duel with Jeffreys, the editor of *The Edinburgh Review*, which affair had become the subject of much banter and had been duly celebrated by me in *English Bards*. Moore, the son of a Dublin grocer, was very fond of issuing challenges to duels, perhaps because it made him feel almost a gentleman. Imagining my insolence of verse insulted him, he had even honoured me with a challenge while I was in foreign parts, but the letter containing this was prudently withheld by my friends. Now he wrote to me again, less belligerently, and, after some inconclusive correspondence, I wrote him a frank and open-hearted letter which led to our meeting at dinner at the house of a third poet, the banker Samuel Rogers. We became fast friends. The only other person present was another poet, Thomas Campbell. This was my introduction to the most famous literary men of my day. Notice I do not say the best. Shelley is that, despite hot air and theories. And Scott, if you discount his politics. While as to Coleridge – I never permit anyone to sneer at *Christabel* in my company; it is a fine wild poem.

At that dinner, I remember Rogers asking me if I would take some soup.

'No, thank you,' I said. 'I never take soup.'

'Ah,' said Rogers, as if he considered this a pretty shrewd investment on my part. 'Some fish then?'

'No, thank you,' I said. 'I never take fish.'

'Ah,' said Rogers, a little less appreciatively, and ordered a plate of mutton to be served.

I did not touch it, nor the cheese, nor the apples.

My fellow poets ate each course with a growing embarrassment.

'A glass of wine?' suggested Rogers.

'No, thank you,' I said. 'I never drink wine.'

Thereupon, in comic despair, and mopping his hard bald dome of a head with a purple silk kerchief, Rogers asked me what I *did* eat and drink.

'Nothing,' I said, 'but dry biscuits and a little soda-water.'

Unfortunately, my amiable host had neither in his pantry, so I was obliged to humour him by dining on potatoes mashed up in my plate and doused with vinegar. I heard later that Rogers happened to meet Hobhouse the next week, and told him this story, adding that in his opinion I must have hurried from his house to my club in order to eat a hearty meat-supper. Hobhouse kindly disabused him. 'So how long will Lord Byron persevere in his strange diet?' Rogers asked. 'Just as long as you continue to notice it,' Hobhouse answered.

My club, incidentally, was the Alfred, a rather dreary, sober, and literary place, which however took the trouble to stock the biscuit I then favoured. I made a point of entertaining both Rogers and Moore there, separately and together, and even Campbell though I liked him less since he was quite unlike his work (which always seems to me a bad sign in a writer). I relished Rogers' sarcasm for a season, until as is always the trouble with malice I perceived how glibly it extended his quite extraordinary egotism. Moore, though a snob, has remained my friend to the present day. Of all the literary types I have known, he has the inestimable merit of being the least *inky*.

Murray, meanwhile, was pressing ahead with the publication of *Childe Harold*. He showed proofs to Rogers, who was then something of an arbiter of fashion in certain literary salons, particularly that of Lady Caroline Lamb (of whom, alas, there will have to be much more in my next chapter). Rogers liked my poem, as I have cause to know, but he was convinced that it would prove a popular failure on account of what he considered its whining tone and its hero's immoral mode of life. Consequently, he praised it to the skies in private, as is the way with writers when they see a new book which they reckon no rival to their own success. Lady Caroline Lamb took this encomium at face value, and spread the word among her tittle-tattle that the young Lord Byron had perpetrated a poetic marvel. To Rogers she said, 'I must meet him!' 'I am dying to meet him!' Whereupon Rogers thoughtfully told her that I had a club foot, and that I bit my nails.

Just a few days before my *Childe* appeared, I made my maiden speech in the House of Lords. The occasion was the second reading of the Nottingham Frame-breakers' Bill, introduced for the purpose of quelling by severe repressive measures the riots among the weavers in opposition to the new machinery which they saw as robbing them of their livelihood. I had seen something of the matter at first-hand when I was at Newstead, where the militia had been called in to crush the workers protesting that the new stocking-frames enabled one man to take the place of seven in every factory. I was perhaps influenced towards anger by the fact that the captain of that local militia was the same brutish Jack Musters whom Mary Chaworth had preferred to me, but in truth I needed no personal motive to speak out on the side of liberty and with a proper sympathy for the oppressed. Adopting the role of a rabid Whig in Lord's clothing, I opposed the Bill with a vigorous speech during the course of which I compared the state of Christian England rather unfavourably with what I had recently seen in the most backward provinces of Turkey. My manner was a sort of modest impudence, and my delivery perhaps a little theatrical, but that is my way: I can say that I meant every impudent, theatrical word. Coming out of the chamber, elated by my own rhetoric, I met Dallas. He had a wet umbrella like a half-dead vulture in his right hand, and therefore proffered only his left with which to congratulate me. I refused it, insisting that he relinquish his vulture and do the job properly.

My speech was something of a triumph, I believe, but any thought I ever had of a career in politics was swiftly cancelled out when this was followed by a far greater triumph in the shape of the publication of *Childe Harold's Pilgrimage*. I trust that there is no need for me to say any more about this matter than that I awoke one morning and found myself famous. Ladies contended for a smile from my lips; editors disputed for a verse from my pen. I was for a season the cynosure of fashionable society – which is to say, the darling of those four thousand odd persons in London who are still up when others are in bed. At the age of twenty-four, in that hectic spring of 1812, I was the man of the moment. And to all this I felt nothing but antipathy. Glory was bitterness to me, and enthusiasm vanity. I drank copious drafts from the silver cup of fame, but I was soon disgusted by the taste, and all the time I knew that it was poison.

CHAPTER TEN

In Which a Literary Lion Lies Down With a Lunatic Lamb

READER, BEWARE! THERE must, I fear, be madness in this chapter; for it was during this period of my raging popularity that there occurred my probably by now quite infamous affair with Lady Caroline Lamb. She was without doubt my evil genius, a necessary angel; and I was, by appointment, her demon lover. Yet I should confess at once, and before descending to the particulars of the case, that my philosophy of Woman is unorthodox to the point of blasphemy against Venus. Despite the part which the sex has played in my life, and the fact that I have been perpetually involved with some of its members, in my heart of hearts I probably despise them, believing as a matter of opinion that they should not be allowed even to eat with men. (I make one sweet exception to this rule and to my despising; *her* I shall come to in good time, when my story demands it, and I find courage equal to my love.) As a general observation, I think that I would not be doing myself much of an injustice if I said that I have treated most of the women I have known with a constant and consistent self-regard. They for their part have been wont to throw first themselves and then the nearest brick at my head. These two things (to the despair of moralists and amorists alike) may not, alas, be unrelated. I once heard it said that Lord Byron had it in him to make some woman very happy. My answer was that a woman had no need of Lord Byron to be happy. It's quite enough to give her a looking glass and a box of sweets.

Lady Caroline Lamb, the only daughter (thank God) of the third Earl of Bessborough, wrote in her journal that I was 'mad, bad, and dangerous to know' even before she had ever spoken half a dozen words with me. She was herself at best a naughty Ariel of a creature, a sprite, a vixen, with a tomboy face crowned with gold hair upswept, a drawling nasally voice, a pretty mouth incapable of truth, big melting eyes with a slight squint in them, and that itch between her legs which always needs scratching. In 1805, at the age of nineteen, this demon had been joined in marriage with William Lamb, second son of Lord Melbourne, a man of some wit but no character. At the point where I came into their story, some seven years later, the happy pair were living under the same roof with Lamb's parents at Melbourne House, in Whitehall. Lady Melbourne, who might have been my mother, was already one of my best and wisest friends, exciting an interest in my feelings that few young women have been able to awaken. She was a charming person – a sort of modern Aspasia, uniting the energy of a man's mind with the delicacy and tenderness of a woman's. I have often thought that, with a little more youth, Lady Melbourne might have turned my head; at all events, she often turned my heart, by bringing me back to mild feelings, when the demon passion was strong within me.

Her daughter-in-law Caroline, an adder in my path, was considered by some no more than a slim little savage of deplorable vivacity. Brought up in luxury and confusion, a child of one of the better families in England, of literary tastes, nervous temperament, and exalted imagination, she had suffered no education to speak of before the age of fifteen, but then a course of misdirected romantic reading and a promiscuous poetic enthusiasm had excited her passions horribly and given her an intense and even voracious desire for love. This incoherent young woman needed adventures as some old men need oysters; she was greedy, capricious, and insatiate. An error of this sort of nature, formed and fed by bad fictions, is a poisoned stream, which overflows the boundary line between the world of poetry and the world of reality. This sylph belonged in a romance where she would certainly have been the heroine. Yet no existing romance was quite ridiculous enough to accommodate her; so eventually she had to resort to writing her own, after having failed in the attempt to live them out. 'I knew I was a fury,' she gave as her reason for at first refusing William Lamb, whom she adored. Partly from upbringing or the lack of it, but more by a precious perversity which was second nature to her, she was missing in anything like balance or self-control. When we first met, at Lady Westmorland's, she turned her back and fled – a clever piece of coquetry, for a bat. A couple of days later, at Melbourne House, I found Rogers and Moore visiting her. She had come in from riding in the park, and flung herself down on a settee without changing her habit. I was announced;

again, she fled. 'Byron,' said Rogers, 'what is your secret? Lady Caroline sits with us in all her dirt, but as soon as she hears your name she runs off to take a bath and make herself beautiful!' I smiled, as I hoped enigmatically, but before long there was not an enigma in sight, only the spectacle of the lady's blazing indiscretions.

I suppose it might be thought dishonourable of me to say so, but Caro's infatuation struck me almost from the start as lunatic. In her very first letter to me she offered me all her jewels, as if she thought by this that she could *buy* me. Adultery was a game of power to her. Having, on the occasion of our third meeting, stilled her feet and *not* fled, she now moved rapidly and continuously in my direction, flinging herself forever into my company, courting me, haunting me, dancing behind and before me like my shadow, hanging upon my every word, pestering me with notes and gifts and kisses. She was in love with the idea of being in love with me. Her heart was like a little volcano, pouring lava through her veins. For my part, I regarded my new mistress as amiable and absurd, perplexing, dangerous, and fascinating. I made her a present of the first rose of that forward spring of 1812, telling her what I had been told, that her ladyship adored all that was new and rare – for a moment. She tried every trick known to woman (and a few known mostly to boys) in her desire to please me, and to please herself with the force and fancy of her own desire. If I let a single day pass without visiting her, she would send me one of her pages with a love-letter written on crazy notepaper whose lace edges formed patterns of shells at each corner of the sheet.

More than once she came herself disguised as a page to bring me such a note, a small androgynous libertine in trousers. There were scenes worthy of *Faublas*. Our intimacy grew until it became the talk of London, which was hardly to be wondered at since all London was reading Caro's diary, one way or another. We would drive home from parties together in my carriage, and before long we came to be *invited* to parties together like husband and wife. Alternatively, if there was a ball, and I happened to be invited on my own, why then Caro would wait about shamelessly in the street for me to come out. It was all very silly and passionate and tiresome and in the end vulgar.

Citizen Matthews (whose own private predilections could have got him to the gallows) used to expound this theory that what a person likes to do in bed tells you a very great deal about their deepest and most secret character. Lady Caroline Lamb liked to tickle and be tickled while I told her stories of how I had buggered boys in the dormitory at Harrow, in silken tents in Albania, out of doors and under the burning stars of Greece. Most of this was of course nonsense which I invented with a glad indifference since it made her hot and happy, but later it cost me dear when she chose for reasons of her own, being then filled with animus against me, to repeat it to my wife and to my wife's lawyers as the gospel truth. For the rest, it will surely be obvious to the reader that two such lovers as we were had no choice but to be engaged head to head in a multiplicity of 'scenes', yet it is with horror and distaste that I have to report that some of these were almost a repetition of those I had enjoyed with my mother – Caro smashing china, throwing salt-cellars and pepperpots, whipping the curtains and the chrysanthemums with her riding crop, shouting and screaming and generally misbehaving in much the same maniacal manner as my father's relict. Of course, thus provoked, I fell back into my own old methods of irritation, bowing and smiling before her tirades, observing each tantrum with a detached and critical coolness, saying very little save for the odd sarcastic comment kept for those moments of her fury which were meant to be the most impressive. There followed tears and repentance on Caro's part, half-contemptuous pardon on mine, and then the inevitable tickling session on the sofa.

For a while, of course, I responded quite gratefully to so much devotion, and was able to extricate myself from the web this sentimental spider wove hectically about me; but then I began to grow tired of it, and bored by her. My passion, such as it had been, perished, consumed in the bonfire of Caro's. It is hard to balance the heat of two hearts when only one of them burns with an inexhaustible flame; the less loving melts like ice before the devotion it can neither comprehend nor return. Also I should confess that I was in this season of my life too much possessed by a spirit of adventure to be willing to give myself up to the worship of one woman, even though that woman wanted to love me to excess. When I tried to break with Caro, I told her plainly that it was not because I loved another, but because loving anyone at all was quite out of my way. I was tired of being a fool, and when I looked back on the waste of my time and the rank destruction of all my plans wrought by our romance, I wanted only to have done with it. I remember remarking to Lady Melbourne, knowing that the sentiment would be passed straight to her daughter-in-law, that in my opinion it was best to make love mechanically, much as one swims without thinking when one falls into water, but that now it was my solemn resolve not to fall into water, and not to make love to anyone until obliged. Caro's response was to send me a big yellow envelope containing cuttings of her pubic hair. I never understood this action, though it smacked of witchcraft, as did a ceremony at Brocket Hall, her family home, where she had an effigy of me burnt in public, while the village girls, in white dresses, danced round the pyre.

Our affair finally came to a head, I suppose, on the occasion when Caro called and, finding me out, scrawled on the front page of the copy of Beckford's *Vathek* which was lying on the hall table: 'Remember me!' On my return, I stood at the table and wrote under these words a fierce *impromptu*:

Remember thee! remember thee!
Till Lethe quench life's burning stream
Remorse and shame shall cling to thee,
And haunt thee like a feverish dream!
Remember thee! Ay, doubt it not.
Thy husband too shall think of thee;
By neither shalt thou be forgot,
Thou false to him, thou fiend to me!

These are cruel and terrible words, I must concede; but I still maintain that they were not untrue. Caro was wounded to the heart when she learned of them, and swore to be avenged. Her dangerous love changed swiftly into hatred. Not being able to use the dagger which would have come naturally to her talent, she took up her pen. Filling her ink-bottle with venom, she poured it out upon my name. She revealed her own shame quite shamelessly to the world. She called her book of vengeance *Glenarvon*, and in it she described me as the Genius of Evil, with all the sweet seduction and innate treachery of the serpent which deceived the first woman. However, her fiction was a lie. In this particular case, I had not been the seducer; if anything, I was the seduced. As for the likeness to me in her wretched *Glenarvon*: the picture can't be good – I did not sit long enough.

The last extravagant scene in this sad history took place one rainy evening in the summer of 1813 when we met by accident at Lady Heathcote's ball. (I say by accident since for my part I would not have attended had I had foreknowledge that Caro was to be there.) What happened then made something of a stir at the time. Lady Heathcote invited Caro to begin the dancing. I believe that she did this because she was embarrassed by the way Caro just stood there staring at me with her squinty eyes. At all events, the invitation made my erstwhile mistress laugh out loud – only her laugh was always too sharp and high for any room she found herself in, and this particular specimen set the chandeliers a-jangling and my teeth on edge. Yet she curtsied prettily to our hostess. 'Oh yes,' she said, 'I'll dance all right! I'm in a merry mood just now!' A young man approached and suggested a waltz as the band struck up; whereupon Caro spun round and called across the assembly to me, 'I conclude that I *may* waltz now?' I smiled and bowed. 'With everyone in turn,' I said, 'why not?' While she was whirling about the floor like a tickled dervish, Lady Melbourne came up with a platter of cheeses and begged me to be kind, but I was beyond kindness. When Caro came sweating prettily back into the room where supper was being served, I remarked how much I had admired her dexterity on the dance floor. She made no reply, but instead seized a knife from the buffet, waving it before me. 'Do, my dear,' I said. 'But if you mean to act a Roman's part, mind which way you strike – be it at your own heart and not at mine.' 'Byron!' she shrieked. Then, because it was expected of her to do *something* no doubt, Caro ran from the room and into an ante-chamber where she succeeded in cutting her hand very slightly, either by accident or design, I don't know which for the life of me, only that her finger got cut and blood came over her gown.

Enough of Lady Caroline Lamb. I don't much like describing people mad, for fear of seeming rather touched myself. I hear that she has now taken to drinking brandy and laudanum, and is in the care of two keepers. Our affair was melancholy, a disaster for which both of us were to blame, though she certainly had the larger share of the suffering. But even that did not teach her any sense.

Talking of suicide attempts, my Margarita just made a rather more impressive pass at one. Under doctor's orders, I showed her the door this morning. Whereupon she stabbed herself with one of her husband's baking implements, and threw herself out of the bedroom window into the canal. Some gondoliers fished her out and returned her to me. It was no good. I lost faith in her from the moment when I discovered that she was learning to read so that she could spy on my letters from others of her sex. Tonight she sleeps again above the bakery, well-compensated for her wounded pride, the limping English milord already assuming the status of a bad dream half-forgotten in that lovely empty head. Her departure means that my various Venetian loves can come and go at random and according to need. In this regard, I have never been happier, or unhappier, I cannot say which.

For some reason now I recall that at the height of my passion for Caro – or, rather, in the deepest depths of her passion for me – I went along one fine May morning to Newgate to see the execution of Bellingham, the lunatic shopkeeper who shot the Prime Minister, Spencer Perceval, in the lobby of the House of Commons. On the way to the hired room overlooking the gallows, our party passed an old witch woman lying drunk in a doorway. When I dropped coins in her lap, she shook her skirts to reject my charity, and then followed us capering down the cobbles in a hideous parody of my crippled gait. I remember her dance rather more clearly than I can remember Bellingham's twitchings at the end of the rope.

These *Memoirs*, it occurs to me, are a relief. When I am tired – and I generally am – out comes this, and down goes everything. Memory is easier than creation. But I can't often bring myself to read over what I've written; so God knows what contradictions all this may contain. Never mind that. St Jude is my patron saint! If I am sincere with myself (but I fear one lies more to one's self than to anyone else), every page should confute, refute, and utterly abjure its predecessor.

In any case, what does it mean – to narrate a life? That it was lived, and that an attempt is being made to raise the dead. And what does it mean – to narrate one's own life? That it still goes on, and that an attempt is being made to prove you are not dead yet. Yet the very act of writing kills the *I* who writes. It was not exactly my first person pronoun that fucked Margarita in the days before she chucked herself in the canal.

CHAPTER ELEVEN

In Which a Poet of Parts Marries a Princess of Parallelograms

Spooney just came here to Venice. I had asked him to bring magnesia (for my indigestion) and red powder and English brushes (for my teeth). Instead, the ancient idiot arrived in a gondola laden only with papers and parchments, having made a great fuss about crossing the mountains and travelling down to me from Geneva. Still, I was glad to see him again, and not least because the purpose of his journey was to obtain my signature for the sale of Newstead to my former Harrow schoolfellow, Thomas Wildman. The price is much lower than Claughton's – ninety thousand guineas – but truth to tell I would have settled for less, the place having been so much trouble in the shape of tenants reluctant to honour their obligations to a landlord in foreign parts. So, Spooney having departed again for London with my signature on the contract, it might be supposed that I am at last about to be once more in funds.

It falls out thus, however:

Owing to moneylenders: £12,000.
Owing to Spooney, his fees: £12,000.

Owing to Lady Byron, the settlement money: £66,000.

Total: £90,000.

So, give or take a guinea or two, I am to have no ready cash as a result of the final sale of my heart, though Spooney was at some pains to inform me that the interest on Lady Byron's settlement will bring me an annual revenue of £3300. If you add to this my income from my poems (in the last two years I have had over £7,000 from John Murray) then I am one of the richer men in Italy. I am glad of that, for in my opinion money is power and pleasure, and I like it vastly. It pleased me, for instance, to be able to send an immediate cheque for £100 to Coleridge a couple of years ago, when I had a begging letter on his behalf, even at a time when I was myself under siege from the bailiffs. How much more generous shall I be able to seem, now that the Newstead toad no longer sits upon me. Playing the rake and the spendthrift was always my way....

My upright downright friend Hobhouse, finding me in bed with two young charmers, once accused me of being a mere rake. The charge rankled. I still consider it untrue. That I am a rake cannot be denied, but I think it only fair to add that there is too much stuff in my head and my heart and certain of my other organs to allow me to be written off as a *mere* rake. Even in my worst days, my literary activity has been immense and intense, and moreover I have always possessed or been possessed by an underlying moral instinct and sense of better things which has refused to be altogether ignored. It is, of course, to this perpetual duality that my personality owes such interest as it may have to others. It finds its best vent in that jumble of flippancy and beauty which is my new poem *Don Juan*, in my opinion by far the truest expression of the esssential man among all my poems. And so, while my loose London life was still in progress, I found my thoughts turning in a general and abstract way towards marriage.

I was conscious of the absolute necessity of redemption, and wedlock seemed to me the obvious way to achieve that blessed state. Without doubt, this idea of marriage was one which, had it been successfully carried out, would have saved me – and that not only from my creditors and literary critics. I arrived at this faith from a careful study of the shortcomings of my past life, and from the imperious promptings of my conscience. A wife, I believed, would be my salvation. Whether the woman has ever existed who would at that or any other period have been equal to the task is a question I cannot presume to answer, in spite of the post-marriage remark of my valet Fletcher, 'Any woman could manage my Lord, except my Lady.' The following lines from a journal I kept in 1813, at which time I was busy turning over possible Lady Byrons in my mind, shows that I, at least, did not consider the idea a hopeless one, though they may convey a different impression to the reader:

'That she won't love me is very probable, nor shall I love her . . . that don't signify. . . . She would have her own way; I am good-humoured to women, and docile; and if I did not fall in love with her, which I should try to prevent, we should be a very comfortable couple. . . . If I love, I shall be jealous; and for that reason, I will not be in love. Though, after all, I doubt my temper . . .

though I should like to have some one now and then to yawn with.'

This notion of myself as one of 'a very comfortable couple' is not without its humour.

We need not trouble with the list of ladies about whom I thought successively (or concurrently) in this connection – enough to say that at one point I was embarrassed between three whom I knew, and one whose name at least I did not know – but we had better come at once to the one to whom the onerous honour fell.

Anne Isabella, shortened by time-saving parents to 'Annabella' and by me to 'Belle', was the only child of Sir Ralph and Lady Milbanke, of Halnaby in Yorkshire and Seaham House in Durham, and a more excellent woman, or one more hopelessly unsuitable as a wife for me, it would have been impossible to find. Besides being an heiress, she was a person of some mental ability, educated with Puritanic strictness, learned in metaphysics and in mathematics, and in her own rather chilly way, quite charming. She had a powerful sense of Christian duty; her few friends were devotedly attached to her; and all her life – a life of martyrdom in her own opinion, I have no doubt – she has remained busily given up to good works, if you can exclude me. Her letters to my sister Augusta after our separation read more like those of a middle-aged woman of the world (in a good sense) to a young and erring sister, than of a girl of four-and-twenty to one some eight years her senior in love's and all other mysteries. It was my sister Augusta – whose shadow fell so darkly and sharply across my wife's life, even as it enriched and sweetened mine – who said of poor Belle in the early days of our marriage, 'I think I never saw or heard or read of a more perfect being in mortal mould than she appears to be.' Oh, my dearest Augusta! This is quite the best and most beautiful sentence which I shall be able to write in this chapter or the next, and the one I have no doubt which will save my sister's immortal soul (not that this particle was ever in any danger in her case). It is a tribute to Augusta also, that she would never at that time or any time afterwards have been able to entertain the notion that the very terms in which she praised Belle were themselves an act of criticism.

You might well imagine that it was precisely that awful perfection, served cold as can be, which was to a great extent responsible for the failure of my marriage. In my own first mention of my future wife you have an illuminating glimpse of the effect which it had upon me. Some of her verses had been submitted to me for appraisal, and while I wrote of them politely, I said of their author, 'She certainly is an extraordinary girl; who would imagine so much strength and variety of thought under that placid countenance? . . . I have no desire to be better acquainted with Miss Milbanke; she is too good for a fallen spirit to know, and I should like her more if she were less perfect.'

Hmm. Let me see. We met first at one of Lady Cowper's receptions. In the entrance to the house I stumbled, and was near falling: a Roman under such circumstances would have returned home; I went in, and saw a young lady, very simply attired, seated on a sofa, with a candid and modest countenance. Her features, though somewhat irregular, were delicate; dark hair, square jaw, level blue eyes, tight mouth; her figure was graceful and flexible; her manner soft and unpretending – affording something of a contrast, indeed, to the artificial manners of English society in that season.

If I possess, as I believe I may do, that greatest quality of genius, frankness, then Miss Milbanke had the peculiarity often found in the feeble, craftiness. I went nearly as far in our early acquaintance as a declaration of love; she went nearly to one of those negatives which excite the passions by declining to deprive them of hope. This gave the semblance of love to my attentions, and to her refined coquetry a certain perfume of victory. A year passed away thus, in doubt and vacillation on my part between the unconquerable aspirations of my nature, which leads me to rush headlong into the world's battles, and the stern counsels of my conscience, which beckons me to the tranquillity of the fireside. The lady, meanwhile, could fairly be said to have had no need of those lacquered marble eggs which were then all the rage among women who favoured such aids to keeping their palms cool in male company.

The first time I proposed to her, she declined. This must have been in the month (October, 1812) when Napoleon began his long retreat from Moscow. Soon after I had my skull examined by Johann Spurzheim, the German phrenologist, who pronounced that all its characteristics were strongly marked and very antithetical, so that my good and evil are at perpetual war. These findings I reported to Miss Milbanke. Our friendship, such as it was, turned into letters. I saw her from time to time at Lady Melbourne's; but I'd other things on my mind, and the problem of Caro. It was about two years later – indeed, after I hadn't set eyes on the woman for some ten months – that I made her what amounted to a second proposal. Why? Well, why not? The sale of Newstead to Claughton had just fallen through. I needed an heiress, and I needed one *quick*. Augusta – with whom I was staying at the time – had been advising me quite strenuously to marry. I was bored and distressed by my life in about equal degrees, so at last I succumbed to my sister's importunings, the only question being: *Whom?* I suggested Miss Milbanke, while Augusta was in favour of another, to whom I recommended that she should write a proposal for me in the first instance. This 'other' (it was Lady Charlotte Leveson-Gower) had the good sense or the good fortune to return a refusal, upon which I remember remarking, 'You see that after all Miss Milbanke is to be the lucky lady; I will write to her.' I did so, notwithstanding the remonstrances of my sister, but the latter, on reading what I had written, observed, 'Well, really, this is a very pretty letter; it is a pity that it should not go – I never read a prettier one.' 'Then go it shall,' said I, and instantly sealed and despatched the sheet and my fate with it.

Thus was poor Annabella seduced and secured by what she herself always describes to others as 'a very beautiful letter'. And such are the perils of literature. When I hear superior liberal persons like Leigh Hunt claim that no one was ever corrupted by the reading of a book, I recall that lovely epistle I wrote Belle, which quite enchanted her mind and befooled her heart. Yet I make myself sound too clever and calculating by half, in admitting to a little epistolary insincerity. Truth to tell, I was a victim too in this exchange, flirting with matrimony for the sake of fine phrases and the feeling a stroke less alone in the world for having a conventional Beloved. O fatal error! Instead of entering the married state with real views of life, I was like one walking in his sleep and murmuring poetry, in danger of stumbling and falling into a bottomless abyss.

An anecdote attaches to the receipt of Belle's reply to this 'beautiful' ugly letter of mine, which reached me a few days later at Newstead. I was at dinner when it came, and a gardener had just handed me my mother's wedding ring, lost by her years before, now found by this honest fellow as he was digging in one of the flower beds. As I took the letter I exclaimed, 'If it contains a consent, I will be married with this very ring!' It did, alas; and I was.

I am only seeking to do myself justice if I choose to emphasise that I manifestly did not marry for money alone – it was salvation of another kind that I was seeking – though I will admit that I perhaps had some idea of escape from *immediate* embarrassments, and had always supposed that my bachelor career would end in my marrying a Golden Dolly or blowing my brains out, it did not much matter which, the remedies being so nearly alike. By the draft of the settlement drawn up by Spooney on the announcement of my impending nuptials, I was to have £1000 a year from my bride's father for my kindness in taking her off his hands, of which I was to allow Belle £300 as pin-money, so that my direct pecuniary gain was only £700, exactly the sum I had to fork out in London for house rent. On my part I settled upon my wife a capital sum of £60,000 secured on the Newstead estate, then valued at £2000 a year. The person who was grasping throughout these necessary transactions was in fact my bride's mother, who soon began squealing for me to make fresh and more vigorous efforts to sell my ancestral home. I remember telling Lady Melbourne that I had taken a considerable and well-informed aversion to my future mother-in-law. At the same time I remember remarking to the same confidant that Belle herself was the most *silent* woman I had ever encountered – something which perplexed me extremely. However, it was not long before I would be wishing for just a bit of that silence back.

Now that I reflect upon it (as I hope for a final time) there seems to me to have been a good deal that is pathetic and an even better deal that is ludicrous in my efforts to persuade myself and others that I had any expectations of happiness from my new condition of betrothal. You may believe that I sincerely wished to play my part fairly and make a good husband, whatever that animal may be, but at the same time I knew from the beginning that my temperament was too strong for me to be one of a happy couple. I was, for example, quite vexedly conscious of the inequality of the marriage settlements; yet, in speaking of them to a friend, I remember saying, 'You know, we must think of these things as little as possible. . . . Bless her! she has nothing to do with it.'

My last bachelor days passed cheerfully enough in London in the company of Tom Moore, who would sit at the piano singing his miserable Irish melodies while I drank brandy. At last, at the start of November,

1814, I stirred myself and set out north for Seaham. To Hobhouse (my best man), with whom I made the journey by post-chaise, I frankly confessed that I was not in love with my intended bride; but at the same time I reported that I felt for her that regard which is the surest guarantee of continued affection and matrimonial felicity. Hobhouse, first meeting Belle at Seaham, told me that he found her dowdy-looking, though (he admitted) she had excellent feet and ankles. For my part, as soon as I set eyes on her again I knew that I had made a mistake. I was marrying a mathematical equation with breasts; a female incarnation of all the deadly virtues.

I can remember discussing gravely with Hobhouse the question of my wedding suit – as to whether I should wear a black coat or a blue one. It was settled on black, as more fitting to my mood. Then, the night before the wedding, I married Hobhouse – which is to say that we had a little rehearsal, in which my old friend appeared in drag in the rôle of the bride. Even this diversion failed to lighten my state of heart and mind. I daresay I was depressed by the discovery that my future father- and mother-in-law found it the height of wit to make endless jokes about fleas and puddings. Fleas on their own I could have stood, but puddings was quite too much for a man of my sensibility.

On the morning of the wedding day, Monday the 2nd of January, 1815, I was filled with the most melancholy reflections on seeing my wedding suit spread out before me like a well-ironed shroud. All the same, I put it on, and ate a hearty breakfast, as befitted a condemned man. Then, to pass the time until the dread stroke of eleven o'clock, I sought, according to my custom, a refuge from trouble in the arms of Mother Nature, so I took a long walk by the sea in one of those English woods at that season leafless, cold, and hopeless as the tomb. The day was harsh and unpleasant. Mists hung over the earth and upon my soul. However, at the hour appointed I went to my doom, which was performed with relish in the drawing-room at Seaham House by the Rev. Thomas Noel, Rector of Kirkby Mallory. Belle was as firm as a rock during the ceremony, though I recall her whispered remark that our wedding-cake made Ossa look like a wart – an observation which I found less than endearing, since it struck me as premeditated playfulness. When she burst into tears after the ceremony I comforted her with the assurance that perhaps we would be as happy as if we had never married at all. What else? Oh yes, Hobhouse remarked to me later that at the words 'with all my worldly goods I thee endow', I looked away from Belle and across at him with a half smile. This seems to me now more likely to give a true impression of my state of mind at the time than the tuppence-coloured picture I painted in my poem *The Dream*, written after the separation, in July of the next year. Odd thoughts of Mary Chaworth may or may not have floated through my mind at that moment – honestly, I cannot now remember one way or the other – but, even if they did, you can be sure that they were very much 'written up' in those melancholy verses.

As I recall it over the intervening years, neither my wife nor myself showed much emotion as we were joined together by that sniffing clergyman, and the only evident histrionics came in the form of the lavish sobbing of my mother-in-law. Hobhouse wore white gloves; Belle a plain gown of white muslin. I do remember that the kneeling-mats did nothing for the rough hard floor of the drawing-room and that the clergyman mistook the pained expression on my face as I knelt before him for a look of religious devotion.

Incidentally, when I came to slip my mother's wedding ring on Belle's finger, I found that it was far too big for her. This was no great wonder, my bride being slim where my mamma had been stout. Belle accepted the discrepancy with grace enough, but Lady Milbanke made a squawking, fluttering and interfering fuss about securing the ring with a band of black ribbon afterwards. This I could not consider a good omen.

For her travelling dress, Belle changed into a slate-coloured satin pelisse with a collar of white fur. We got into the carriage. It was snowing. I remember that good old decent Hobby ran along beside the vehicle as it moved away down the drive, grasping my hand through the open window, reluctant to let me go. Then he was gone, and Belle and I were alone together at last. She said nothing. I saw that her cheeks were bright with tears. As I always do when I am unhappy, I burst into song. 'What language is that?' Belle asked. 'Why, Greek, of course,' I answered. The cathedral bells rang as we rode through the city of Durham. 'They ring for our happiness,' said Belle. 'Or our doom,' I said, and sang on. The song wasn't Greek, but Albanian.

This journey to Halnaby, where what I called our 'treaclemoon' was to be spent, proved only too typical of the longer, though, as it transpired, not very much longer, journey upon which the ill-assorted pair of us had now set out. We stopped at an inn in Rusheyford and I ate an omelette. Belle sat twisting her napkin in her lap and staring at the fire. Neither of us had anything to say that would cover the situation. When we got back into the carriage I felt too dispirited even to sing.

It was dark, thank God, when finally we came to Halnaby Hall. I was half frozen stiff, and the courtyard was full of geese gaggling in the snow. I remember that the servants made a fuss of Annabella, especially a cross-eyed butler and a maid called Mrs Minns who escorted us up the stairs to our nuptial chambers with a candle in each paw. The rooms faced north over the snow-bound meadows. Fires blazed in each of them but did little to dispel the cold. I noted that the beds had damask curtains.

I believe that it was at this point that I said something unforgivable to Belle to the effect that it was now too late, that she could have saved me if she had accepted me the first time I had asked for her hand, but that now there was no remedy for my condition: something irreparable had happened, and in due course she would come to realise that she had married a devil. I meant these remarks very seriously, as you shall learn when I come to the story of the one true object of my heart's affections. At this point, though, it may perhaps be appropriate if the reader finds himself or herself as baffled and perplexed by my dark hints as poor Belle was on the night of our wedding.

When I saw the consternation written on her face, I laughed and pretended I'd been joking. The truth, I am afraid, was that now I held this pathetic princess of parallelograms in my power, and I desired above all else to make her feel it. At the moment of going to bed, I asked her if she intended to sleep in the same bed as me. 'I hate sleeping with any woman,' I remember saying to her, 'but you may if you choose.' She chose, and the night passed pleasantly enough, though my bride turned out to be a virgin and quite hard work besides. I had her on a sofa in the sitting room before taking her education a little further between the sheets. Surprisingly, in view of her coolness when upright and her passion for statistics, I found Belle not averse to her conjugal duties. Our treaclemoon was not exactly a catastrophe. She copied out my poems in the mornings and I taught her new ways of making couplets rhyme each night. In the early stages of her sexual apprenticeship, to be sure, it was not unknown for her to munch at an apple with her face turned sideways on the pillow, while I was working away below like a galley-slave, and on one awful occasion she even found it in herself to enquire 'Have you finished?' when I hadn't. Before our weeks at Halnaby were at an end, however, I succeeded in introducing this most unsportive of women to the delights of congress in the Italian style – which is to say that I buggered her. As a matter of fact, I think I may claim that Lady Byron enjoyed my doing this even more than she enjoyed the attentions of my cocker at the other entrance, and it is my opinion that it must have come as a considerable shock to her when her marital lawyers later gave her the advice that the act constituted a criminal offence. One of the fondest memories I have of our times together at Halnaby is of Belle bent over that same sofa where I had first had her, a velvet cushion pressed into her little belly, her dress up, her drawers down, and her bottom cheeks clenching and unclenching with shivers of anticipation as she awaited the updriving of my prick. . . . The remembrance of that, no doubt, tends to impart a more sombre hue than it might otherwise have borne to a really absurd incident which marked the night of our wedding day. Waking from my first sleep in the strange surroundings, in a half-dazed condition of mind, I saw the fire which burned in the grate glowing through the crimson curtains of the marriage bed. 'Good God!' I cried. 'I am surely in Hell!'

After a stay of just under three weeks at Halnaby, we returned to Seaham House, where we remained another six, and where I was woefully bored in the evenings by Sir Ralph's indulgence in that damnable monologue which elderly gentlemen are pleased to call conversation. I remember that he told interminable anecdotes about clergymen of his acquaintance, mostly bishops. Having little enough in that line to offer by way of return, I regaled him nevertheless with the story of how Lady Caroline Lamb had once risen from the dinner table to ask her husband, 'George, what is the seventh commandment?' 'Thou shalt not bother,' said George Lamb. My father-in-law professed himself amused by this, but I noticed that his beady eyes went to and fro as though he half-expected a hobgoblin to emerge from behind the fire-irons and carry me off to Halifax or even more infernal regions.

It was only after a visit to my sister Augusta at her house Six Mile Bottom, near Newmarket, that Belle and I went up to London, to Number 13, Piccadilly Terrace, which was to be our home during the rest of our brief life together —

But I am quite worn out with these ambrosial reminiscences of my princess of parallelograms. It may well be true that as I once said to her very early in our acquaintance, the great object of life is sensation, to feel that we exist, even though in pain. But presently I feel nothing but weariness, and desire an end of it. I can hear my valet Fletcher snoring like a pig in the next room. I think I'd better emulate his example.

First, though, as always before I sleep, a dream in verse:

Ah, fatal hour, that saw my prayer succeed,
And my fond bride enact the Ganymede.
Quick from my mouth some bland saliva spread
The ingress smoothed to her new maidenhead,
The Thespian God his rosy pinions beat,
And laughed to see his victory complete.
'Tis true, that from her lips some murmurs fell –
In joy or anger, 'tis too late to tell;
But this I swear, that not a single sign
Proved that her pleasure did not equal mine.
Ah, fatal hour! for thence my sorrows date:
Thence sprung the source of her undying hate.
Fiends from her breast the sacred secret wrung,
Then called me monster; and, with evil tongue,
Mysterious tales of false Satanic art
Devised, and forced us evermore to part.

CHAPTER TWELVE

Nine Months of Domestic Bliss at 13 Piccadilly Terrace

Today is my birthday, the thirty-first of its kind. I have celebrated this event by completing a second canto of my new poem, *Don Juan*, and instructing Murray to print fifty copies of Canto One of the same for private circulation. Hobhouse and other friends in England have advised me against a general publication on the grounds that the work will give offence because of what they call 'attacks' on my wife and also 'the bawdry and the blasphemy'. I will not make any alterations to what I have written, nor allow a single line to be cut on moral grounds, so there's an end of it. Given all this, it is perfectly plain to me that the present *Memoirs* will never see the light of day during my lifetime either, and perhaps not afterwards even. My truest work is now unfit for publication; Amen. I have stomach trouble. I have signed a codicil to my will providing a legacy of £5000 for my daughter Allegra. It is Carnival time again in Venice and for the past ten days I have not been in bed until seven or eight in the morning. Just to add to my other troubles and afflictions, let me set it down here that I am also damnably in love with the queerest woman I ever met, a nineteen-year-old countess from Ravenna called Teresa Guiccioli, who is married to a fellow in his fifties. How pleasant it is to make love in a curtained gondola to a girl from the city where Dante lies buried. Shelley just met her and pronounced her in his opinion a definite improvement not only on Margarita but on the hired *ragazzi* that took Margarita's place. My ardent little countess, says the author of *Queen Mab*, is 'sentimental, innocent, and superficial.' So she is, and that will do for me.

Over the story of my separation from my wife I must now hasten with what speed I can muster. From the very day of the wedding I found myself on the way to the separation. 'What a fool I was to marry!' I remarked to Hobhouse on meeting him again in London, and with this sentiment, which was the key-note of my lamentations from first to last, I am still inclined to sympathise and agree. I am essentially, as Scrope once noted, a man's man, and my habitual attitude to women can be tersely and frankly summed up. I regard them as very pretty and entertaining but inferior creatures who are as little in their place at our tables as they would be in our council chambers. The whole of the present system with regard to the female sex seems to me no more than a remnant of the barbarism of the chivalry of our forefathers. I look on the female sex as grown-up children; but, like a foolish mamma, I am constantly the slave of one of them. The Turks shut up their women, and are much happier; if all else fails, there is always the sack and the Bosphorus. To tell you the truth, though it may be heretical, I have not quite made up my mind that women have souls.

Among my affections is the no doubt ridiculous one

of deep aversion to seeing a woman eat. (Yet this, I must maintain, is in itself no more absurd than Dean Swift's surprise that one of the fair number should shit.) All the same, given my aversion, and other sensitivities of the sort, what hope could there be of my achieving matrimonial happiness with anyone, let alone with a partner so little fitted to playing the beautiful slave as the former Miss Pythagoras of Halnaby Hall? Men seek perfection in the object of their love; women, imperfection. But in this case each of us found rather too much of the usual *desideratum* in the other. Belle's views on life were as formed and correct as mine were lax and intuitive, and she lived up to her expectations of the world consistently, if a trifle too consciously for my taste. She was, most literally, too good for me. It was of course impossible for me to hold such a creature in indulgent contempt, and this may well have added to the bitterness of my consciousness that I was sadly failing to carry out the good resolutions with which I must in fairness be credited. The short year spent in Piccadilly Terrace was a year of steadily increasing misery. Utter and hopeless incompatibility was at the root of it. Lady Byron's first idea was always what was due to herself. I wished all the time that she could think just a little more of what was due to others, including me. My besetting sin, I suppose, was a want of that self-respect which she had in excess. When I broke out, on slight provocation, into one of my ungovernable fits of rage, her calmness piqued and reproached me; it gave her an air of superiority that vexed and increased my *mauvaise humeur*. For her, the highest level lovers could attain was mutual esteem; for me, it was mutual orgasm. Meanwhile, of course, the world went its own way with no regard for the state of sameness and stagnation that was our marriage. Napoleon came back to France and I joined the sub-committee of management of Drury Lane Theatre.

At first, things might not have looked too bad, to Boney's eye, say, or Edmund Kean's. We had a staff of servants and two carriages, though bailiffs did for most of the furniture as the year wore on. The fact that *The Siege of Corinth* and *Parisina* were both copied out for the publisher in my wife's fair hand speaks for itself, as in a less degree does the reflection that the period was one of considerable literary activity, for, besides the two longer works, in it were written *There's not a joy the World can give*, *We do not curse thee Waterloo*, *Must thou go, my glorious Chief?*, *Star of the Brave*, and *Napoleon's Farewell* – not a contemptible output for a few months, filled as those months were with distractions of an unpoetical nature. As to the world of literature, I met at last Sir Walter Scott, perhaps the only living writer for whom my esteem and admiration is unbounded, and I rode on a piebald rocking-horse with Leigh Hunt's children while their father preached to me of Castlereagh. I remember the flickery wisdom of Scott's smile when he remarked that he thought my opinions on politics and religion would change as I grew older. 'I suppose,' I said, 'you are one of those who prophesy that I'll turn Methodist?' 'No,' said Scott, 'I don't expect your conversion to be of such an ordinary kind. I would rather look to see your retreat upon the Catholic faith, and distinguish yourself by the austerity of your penances. The species of religion to which you must, or may, one day attach yourself must exercise a strong power on the imagination.' He gave me a dagger, mounted in gold, which was once the property of Elfi Bey. It sits beside me now on this manuscript of my *Memoirs*.

Not long before the Battle of Waterloo there was a meeting between Lady Caroline Lamb, well-powdered, and Lady Byron, encumbered with virtue, at the house of one or the other, I cannot now remember which, for the life of me. Wherever the visit was paid, it was, as may easily be understood, not marked by any exuberant geniality on either side. I was told that Caro claimed to have shaken hands with me on this occasion, and that she found my hand cold, though I seemed kind. If that is truly so, then I must have been drunk or drugged, but for my part I doubt it. Belle's comment on Caro was, 'Such a wicked-looking cat I never saw.'

Money troubles, those potent solvents of domestic bliss, were very much in evidence from the outset of our union. In the nine months we lived at Piccadilly Terrace there were I think no fewer than nine executions in the house, and you can hardly wonder at the irritation caused by the all-too-perfect Annabella when she glided into the room where I, her lord, was stood before the fireplace brooding over our embarrassments, and she came out with the futile question, 'Am I in your way, Byron?' '*Damnably!*' I said. Well, so she was.

My work on the management committee of Drury Lane Theatre did not add to the connubial peace. I was not the sort of husband whose wife would approve of being frequently brought into contact with the ladies of the stage, one of whom, Claire Clairmont, became the mother of my little illegitimate Allegra, though I may point out that I bedded the bitch only when she flung herself at me, and that this miserable weekend's rutting occurred *after* the separation from Belle. As to pregnancy, by the time of Waterloo my wife was three months advanced in the condition. Had this not been the case, then I might well have journeyed with Hobhouse to France, to follow the fortunes of the armies. 'Poor fellow!' he said, when he heard that Napoleon had been beaten. My sentiments exactly.

Hobby came back. Murray annoyed me by saying that he had felt safe in reading my latest works aloud to Mrs Murray, since he had recognised the delicate hand that had copied them out. A bailiff took to sleeping in the house. I blamed Belle when this lout cast greedy looks at my library. She looked down her nose and passed the observation that bailiffs were quite the subject of my romance these days. So it went on. Spring passed, summer passed, autumn came and the usual fogs seeped up from the river. In the last weeks of Belle's pregnancy I added to my other delinquencies that of laudanum-drinking. I liked the ruby glow of the fat little bottle in the evening on the mantleshelf. I read somewhere of an English gentleman who retired to bed for the winter with only his bottle of laudanum for company; that seemed to me at the time an admirable stratagem. The firelight glowed, cinders fell from the grate and smouldered on the carpet and I could not bring myself to bother to kick them out, sprawled as I was in a deep chair, turning the pages of Coleridge's *Christabel*. My conduct was in many respects brutally inconsiderate and neglectful. I insisted upon taking all my few meals alone, and would spend days on end in sulky silence. My one good deed, you might say, was that in November I wrote to Murray and told him to publish the Coleridge. He did this the following year; one of my small services to English poetry, which I record now in desperation that the rest of my existence in this bleak period must seem so black. Also, it was at my urging that Coleridge published *Kubla Khan.* You can say what you like about me, but when you have finished set down this: He knew a true poem when one read him.

As Belle's confinement drew near, she began to entertain strong doubts of my sanity and to fear for her personal safety. Her tranquillity was not enhanced by my habit of keeping loaded pistols in the bedroom, though I always considered this myself a mark of responsibility. One night I came in drunk from my carriage and appeared to be overwhelmed with remorse. Calling myself a monster and so forth, I threw myself in agony at Belle's feet, and rolled about a bit, and howled, and wept. Astonished by this resurgence of virtue (as she supposed), the poor thing was completely taken in. Tears of joy and pity flowed down over her face, and she exclaimed, 'Byron, all is forgiven! Never, never shall you hear of it more!' Then I sat up, folded my arms across my chest, and burst into laughter. 'What do you mean?' my wife cried, still further amazed. 'Merely a philosophical experiment,' I explained, 'that's all.' When Belle continued blank, I reminded her that only that morning she had taken a vow never to speak to me again unless I withdrew some reference to her being a mathematical formula in buttoned gloves, which needless to say I wouldn't.

'I wished only to ascertain the value of your vows,' I said.

I suppose I must acknowledge that the woman was most sorely tried. However, it is not true that during her hours of labour I threw empty champagne bottles at the ceiling to annoy her; nor did I fire off my pistols in the room below her confinement as she later claimed. The truth is merely that I had at that period a bad habit of employing a poker to knock off the tops of my bottles of soda-water, and the reports which came to Belle's ears in the bedroom above were no more than the result of this innocent if thoughtless activity. Our daughter Ada was born on the tenth of December, 1815, despite her mother's fears and her father's fancies. I loved that child from the moment I saw her and I love her still. However, Ada's entrance into this world came too late to keep her parents together. Perhaps it was always too late for that, from the beginning of Time?

I saw Lady Byron for the last time on an evening in the middle of January, 1816, almost exactly one month later. She walked into the room where I was sitting with Augusta, and she held out her hand, and she said, 'I have come to say good-bye, Byron.' I think that I folded my arms. Certainly, I stood up, and walked to the fireplace, and leaned upon the mantelshelf with my cheek against the cool rotundity of the laudanum bottle. Then I turned and looked with a smile from my wife to my sister. 'And when,' I said prettily, 'shall we three meet again?'

'In heaven, I trust,' said Annabella, and went.

CHAPTER THIRTEEN

(X X X)

I SHALL BEGIN this sweetest, most secret, bitterest, deepest, darkest, most difficult and demanding of the chapters in the story of my heart, by asking the reader to peruse a poem of mine which it is not my intention ever to publish otherwise. I request only that it be read with care and attention, and for truth's sake, which is how it was written:

I speak not – I breathe not – I write not that name –
There is grief in the sound, there is guilt in the fame. . . .
We have loved – and oh, still, my adored one we love!
Oh the moment is past, when that Passion might cease. –
We repent, we abjure, we will break from the chain, –
We will part, we will fly to – unite it again! . . .
The thought may be madness – the wish may be guilt!
Forgive me, adored one! – forsake, if thou wilt; –
But I cannot repent what we ne'er can recall. . . .
And stern to the haughty, but humble to thee
The soul in its bitterest moments shall be. . . .
And thine is that love which I will not forgo
Though the price which I pay is Eternity's woe.

Inchoate? unpolished? lacking all my usual sparkle? Yes, yes, and yes, but the these lines were wrung from my heart, and go against all reason and discretion. I wrote them in the May of 1814. Their subject, their object, the ground of their being, is my only true love: my sister Augusta.

I had seen Augusta – my father's only child by his first wife, Lady Carmarthen – from time to time when she visited me at Harrow, and came for her holidays to Newstead. But in the sense of that poem, in the spirit which grips me now, Augusta first really came into my life in the summer of 1813. I was twenty-five, famous, bored by my fame, still reeling from Caroline Lamb. She was four years my senior, amusing, flighty, kind, in search of distractions no doubt after several years of marriage to an oaf. But, oh, oh, dearest Guss, little goose, sweetest Sis, how can I set down your arrival on my doorstep in London as if it were simply another chronological event between, say, my affair with the libertarian Lady Oxford, who burst a blood vessel every time I poked her at Eywood, and my crass ambition at that time to forsake the muddy pool of my own fame and obtain a passage in a ship of war and sail off into another Mediterranean sunset? I'll tell you how it was, for my own pleasure. And my own pain, besides. I remember, as if it was yesterday, your sudden appearance in my Bennet Street apartments, in the early afternoon of Sunday, June 27th. (I dearly love a date, and celebrate this one.) You were wearing a coat of blue velvet lined with white silk, and a blue velvet hat with an ostrich plume in it. You were shy and wild and careless of your appearance, with the pouting lips and frowning brows of all the Byrons, and when you spoke the first thing I noticed was that like me you never could bother to bring yourself to pronounce an 'r'. From the start, I think, I fell in love with your voice, not just what you said, though I found that infantile prattle, that damned crinkum-crankum, ineffably sweet and endearing to listen to but, oh, the very rise and fall, the crazy liveliness, the fine childish incoherence of your talk. Yes, it was your way of talking that first and most enchanted me. *The Augustan Mysteries*, I called it.

I recall, at that original meeting, you asked out of politeness or convention if I had any new verses which you might see; and I replied that even if I read them to you, you would not understand them; and you laughed, not at all insulted or put down, in fact *satisfied*, a laugh of pure satisfaction that I had called your bluff, and that some queer essential sense of the comical and nonsensical had been recognised in you. Before long that summer you were calling me Baby B., and I addressed you as my Sister Goose. It will sound asinine to anyone else, but to us the silly names themselves were a key to a nursery world of make-believe in which we could play at husbands and wives, as children do, only we did what children cannot.

We made love in Bennet Street, yes; we were star-crossed, and itching with curiosity, and we couldn't stop ourselves. But in London you were shy and we had to be careful. That next autumn and winter in the country is what I remember. You'd told me of your house, the dismal manor, set in a copse of black yew-trees, the place where you said nothing happened and never would happen. Six Mile Bottom! Well, we made something happen there, didn't we? Six Mile Bottom! The house of incest! If I shut my eyes now I can still see the light of the flames which shone on the silver tea-pot and danced in your mischievous brown eyes, and if I stop my ears I shall hear again the sound of shutters banging, banging in the wind, and then later – when the wind had dropped – we stood together and watched from the wide window as the snow fell, thick snow, softly falling snow, more snow than I ever saw fall in a single hour. We put on our cloaks and our boots and we walked in the snow with your spaniels, and we ran, and threw snowballs at each other, and you stood under the bare branches of the oak with red cheeks and with icicles on your eyelashes, and you took my arm and said that when you were a little girl you always liked to think of Ulysses having a limp. Dear Guss. It was all so easy and good and I daresay we slipped into sensuality as sweetly and unthinkingly as any lovers ever did, the whole affair made more convenient (yet also at the same time given spice) by the fact that our relations were so strangely familiar. We had not been brought up together under the same roof in the innocence of childhood. My father was your father, but my mother was not your mother. I could claim, then, in defence of what we did, that you were only my *half* sister, and that because our childhoods had been spent quite separately there was never anything unnatural or illicit about our love. Yet if I said that, would I not be denying that one of the spurs which drove me into your arms, and tempted you to want me between your sheets, was the very sweet erotic fact that our commerce was incestuous and forbidden? Once the thought struck me, the idea of incest haunted and possessed me. Were we not both Byrons, and are not the Byrons as splendid, damned, and doomed as any

Borgias? I was always fascinated by the possibility of the sin against the Holy Ghost, the unpardonable crime that would set me above and beyond all law, both human and divine. I found it – oh so darkly and deliciously – that snow-bound night at your house in the middle of nowhere, when we sat on the floor in front of the fire in the library, and I took your hands in my hands to kiss your fingertips, and you stroked my hair, and when I whispered in your ear you laughed your scatterbrain laugh, and we went up the stairs together, quick as we could, still whispering and laughing, hand-in-hand, like a wicked Hansel and a wanton Gretel, to tear off each other's clothes and fall into your bed and make love.

So there it is, put briefly and bluntly, the heart of the great 'Byron mystery', as Hobby used ironically to call it. Did Hobby guess the truth? Like enough he did, and he was not the only person who knew, since in one of those unguarded moments of self-damaging self-revelation which have plagued me all my days (and is not this present writing just such another?) I went and told Lady Melbourne, that tolerant improvement on my mother, most if not all of the shocking lovely truth about us. Guss, Goose, forgive me that, sweet Sis. Be sure that I said that *you* were not to blame, not one thousandth part in comparison with me, made by God for my own misery, no less. I stressed that you were not aware of your own peril until it was too late.... Yet why, save for the relish which the very notion of incest gives to the joys of the flesh, why should I now be ashamed of what we did? You are the only one who has truly loved me and whom I have truly loved. Part of my horribleness to Caro, and most of my vileness towards Belle, came from the fact that they simply were not you; that I see now with an overwhelming clarity. August Augusta, my A., my dearest (X X X) ——— there! I have written down here the mark which was between us the secret sign of our love for each other; the cipher of our bliss; our signature of incest. I should have had the courage to insist that you left gormless George, and your three children, and ran away with me to Greece or Sicily. Alas, when I mentioned that project to Lady Melbourne, swearing her to secrecy, that most unshockable of women was shocked to the core. 'Byron,' she told me, 'you are on the brink of a precipice. If you do not retreat, you are lost forever.' So, fool that I was, like Napoleon, I did retreat. I pretended to love first this one and then that. I used first the idea and then the fact of marriage to mask our incest. Anything rather than let the world know for certain that your brother was the father of the child with which you were already pregnant by that Christmas of 1813.

And yet, of course, I half-wanted the world to know.... In the grip of a compulsion, I wrote in four nights that November my poem *The Bride of Abydos*, a dark delicious flaunting of the incest theme, in which my Zuleika and Selim are half-sister and half-brother, offspring like us of the same father but different mothers. Had I not written it, I must have gone mad, by eating my own heart in secret – O bitter diet! I believe that the composition of it kept me alive from the perpetual recollection of your dear sacred name, my dearest Augusta. And then, three weeks after this poem was published, I began *The Corsair*, finishing it in ten days, a poor enough piece (though I heard 10,000 copies were sold on the day of its publication, and 15,000 more in the month that followed); a poor enough piece, though, I say, but with one important connection with our own story. At the time I was writing it, you were carrying our child; and when that child was born we christened her Medora, after my heroine. Such namings are poetry; they reveal and conceal in the same breath. (My child by Lady Byron, in full, is *Augusta* Ada.)

Poor Medora! Poor Augusta! Poor us! But it makes me laugh now, albeit bitterly, to remember that old Lady Melbourne, a superstitious soul in a liberal frame, actually predicted in my hearing that the fruit of our incestuous union was bound to be a monster. Well, it was not an ape, after all, was it, dear Goose? How could it be, with an angel for a mother and a devil for a father? Yet we had to be wise and prudent, in our fashion. I stayed away from Six Mile Bottom after Medora's birth. I did not see you again until high summer. I went back to my boxing and my fencing; I frequented the theatres. That was the season of Kean's great *Othello*, and some actress whose name I cannot now recall who played Cleopatra much as Shakespeare must have intended her. And it struck me again how great a genius that Shakespeare was – to have created his Cleopatra without the benefit of knowing you! Because when I watched that magic on the stage at Drury Lane it was you I was seeing, you, you, you, the epitome of your sex – fond, lively, sad, tender, teasing, humble, haughty, beautiful, the devil! Augusta's infinite variety, which cannot stale. Coquettish to the last, my dear sister, as well with the asp as with Mark Antony or me. And it must have been then that I sent you my portrait, and you, who had once so feared my love that you said you couldn't breathe when I reached out with trembling fingertips to touch your nipples, you sent me back a small white packet with a lock of your dear hair in it, and with this note in French:

> *Partager tous vos sentiments,*
> *ne voir que par vos yeux,*
> *n'agir que par vos conseils, ne*
> *vivre que pour vous, voilà mes*
> *voeux, mes projets, et le seul*
> *destin qui peut me rendre*
> *heureuse.*

Dearest darling adorable Goose, to share all *your* feelings, to see only through *your* eyes, to act only on *your* advice, and to live only for *you* – those were and are *my* vows and *my* projects also, and the sole destiny that could ever have made *me* happy, too. Only now I am cut off from that destiny by more than time and distance. I am denied your face, your talk, your company. All that I possess is this lock of your hair, still shining from the gorgeous silly glory that is you. I take it and I twine it in my fingers now, as I write, La Chevelure of the *one* whom I most loved. O my dear, my dear, a love like ours is quite impossible. No doubt it does not belong in this benighted world at all. Sometimes I think that such love comes from elsewhere, and takes up residence in us, and uses us, and discards us when it has done with us. As if the moon fed on the creatures of the earth, and all dull sublunary lovers had nothing to do but satisfy her appetite. I am at my philosophising again, as you see, sweet Sis, but tonight the very philosophy of such a love as ours seems to me so dreadful in its implications that I doubt whether even you could shake me from my stupor of sin and regret. The kind of feeling which has lately absorbed me has a mixture of the terrible, which renders all other insipid to a degree; in short, one of its effects has been like the habits of Mithridates, who by using himself gradually to poison of the strongest kind, at last rendered all others ineffectual when he sought them as a remedy for all evils, and a release from existence. If there's a cure for love, it is not called Augusta.

Well then, now then, I have used the word *regret*, and that constitutes a swelling of the truth, if not a lie. Because what I should say is that it was our love affair which accomplished what had been heretofore impossible: in making love to you, I shocked myself, a delightfully fresh sensation. I remember remarking to Tom Moore, sometime in that you-soaked summer of 1813, that I was involved in a far more serious scrape than any which had bestirred my heart from the start. But Moore, for all his mellifluousness, has the soul of a grocer at bottom, and certainly he guessed nothing of the facts. And you, my Goose, what did you think of it all? Mostly you laughed and you sighed, but you never said anything direct upon the subject. When I try to imagine what effect your complicity in the act of incest had upon your own soul, all I can think of are the crimson spots in your cheeks, and your hot hand upon my cocker. Do you remember when we carved our initials on that tree stump at Newstead? That was of course the very afternoon that I wrote the letter to Annabella, asking her to marry me.... Marriage seemed to both of us a way to make light of our darkness, a necessary escape from the sort of scandal which otherwise must have engulfed us. Yet, oh, how different my days with you at Newstead and at Newmarket, how utterly opposite to my life with the connubial equation! *We* never yawned or disagreed, did we, Guss? And we laughed very much more than was suitable to those ancestral halls, the family shyness of the Byrons making us far more amusing companions to each other than either of us ever could prove to anyone else. Details. Let's see. I gave you lessons in Italian. You learned all my fears and my shortcomings – how I grind my teeth in my sleep like a bulldog, so that sometimes it is necessary for me to stuff a napkin between my jaws to prevent me from biting myself; how when I'm sleepless I choose to drink soda-water all night long, twelve bottles at a time being nothing to me, knocking the heads off the bottles with a poker, or shooting them off with my pistol, the better to amuse you; how I am quite as hopeless a trichomaniac as John Milton, and loved nothing more than to sit by you while you brushed your hair. . . . You let me; you seemed to adore to allow me to watch you at your toilet – we sat there in front of the looking-glass like two twins in love. And kissing your lips was like kissing my own lips made female.

That year that Medora was born, I was twenty-six. Six hundred in heart – and in head and pursuits about six. . . . Still, at twenty-six, when all is said and done, one ought to be something. But what was I? Who loved me? Only you. Who knew me? Only you. That year my poem *The Corsair* was published; it sold, as I've already boasted, 10,000 copies on the day of publication, a thing perfectly unprecedented, as Murray was delighted to point out to me. As for its author, he went to Covent Garden and sat solitary in his private box; or he dined (on fish alone) with Rogers or Sheridan, and tried not to show that he was bored to the boots by their society now. Hobhouse observed that I was growing into a *loup-garou*, a solitary hobgoblin. I began another set of verses, *Lara*, in which for once my hero didn't visit foreign parts. My Lara belonged to no time and no place in particular; he was the hero alone; he was myself. I remember that there were four lines in it which you learned by heart, little goose, and quoted back at me for ever after:

There was in him a vital scorn of all:
As if the worst had fall'n which could befall,
He stood a stranger in this breathing world,
An erring spirit from another hurl'd. . . .

Clever of you to fix on that, I think. I never painted a truer portrait of my innermost being. But you too, Augusta, you share it with me that you do not belong either in this breathing world; you are the second erring spirit; my other self. Therefore I loved you. Wherefore I still do.

Belle knew, of course. Well, shall we say that she both knew and did not want to know, and that in that calculating machine which she called her mind she managed sometimes to suppress and sometimes to admit the terrible information. The information, I mean, that her husband was not in love with her, had never been in love with her, would not ever be the very least part in love with her. The knowledge that her husband was in love with his sister; had bedded his own sister; wanted nothing else, having tasted the forbidden fruits of incest, than to return again to his sister's arms and lay down his head on her breast. I recall that the very first morning of my marriage, when I woke at Halnaby, there was a letter from you on the breakfast table, and I tore it open with a kind of gloating frenzy, and read it aloud to Annabella, especially the salutation: '*Dearest, first, and best of human beings....* – Now, what do you think of that?' I asked Lady Byron.

What precisely she thought of it, I never quite did know. I confess that I took a hideous cruel pleasure in tormenting poor Belle with hints. It was as if I dared her always to ask me what it was that I could not tell her. Once, when she spoke to me of Dryden's *Don Sebastian*, a veritable tragedy of incest, I burst into a rage and told her never even to mention the name of such a work again. At night, she saw me racked with dreams and nightmares. 'You should have a softer pillow than my heart,' I said to her, one night. And Belle answered: 'I wonder which will break first, yours or mine?'

Dearest Augusta, sweetest Sis, it was to you, naturally, and to your house at Six Mile Bottom, that I brought myself and my wife when at last we left Seaham. I believe we intended to stay just a day or two. In the event, as you know, we stayed for the whole of that March. You were kindness itself. As for me, I drank brandy and made devilish remarks to Lady Byron. The three of us were sitting in the library, late, and I advised her to retire. 'We don't need *you*, my charmer!' That's what I said. Later, up in the marital bedroom, I went further: 'Now that I have *her*, you'll find that I can do without *you* – in all ways!' I slept in my cloak on the sofa. I was dazzled with drink; I was tired and confused and terrified by the power of my own feelings now that I had seen you again, had seen you beside her, had seen for a fact that I'd married her because our love was futureless.... These are reasons explaining the causes of my cruelty, but of course they do not excuse it. One night I quoted to you, in front of her, that most secret of my poems: '*We repent, we abjure, we will break from our chain....*' Perhaps Belle didn't see I was still burning for your bed? But she *must* have comprehended perhaps the most wicked of my verbal actions, when I bent over Medora's cradle, and turned to her and said, '*You know this is my child?*'

I took Belle on to London; we set up house together at Number 13, Piccadilly Terrace. Did she not consider it a touch strange that there was an interval of only ten days before you came tripping up to town and moved in with us? We were ten days apart, and then ten weeks together. I heard later that my wife told one of her lawyers that she considered it hopeless to keep us apart; but not hopeless, in her opinion, to keep us innocent. 'I felt myself the guardian of those two beings,' she said. As for me, I made no bones about my pleasure in seeing you. And I told Belle that she was a fool for letting you come into the house. 'You'll find it will make a great difference to *you* in all ways,' I said. She found out soon enough what it was I meant. Then she wanted to kill you. Imagine that: Lady Byron, the celebrated murderess! She admitted there were times then when she was almost mad. So to prevent herself in indulging the passion of revenge, she was obliged to substitute another – that of romantic forgiveness. Unfortunately, my wife's eventual forgiveness extended only to you. I daresay I deserved no less, Augusta.

I was a man living a nightmare all that hellish year of my marriage. I sent you away at the end of June; in August I followed after you to Six Mile Bottom; you sent me back to London, to my pregnant parallelogram. The next few months were as bad as any in my life. Blame it on the laudanum. Blame it on the battle of Waterloo. Sometimes it seemed to me that another Byron stepped out of the mirror and did the things I saw. One night, in a fit of fury, while Annabella looked on helpless, I threw a clock on the floor and struck it again and again with the poker until it was smashed. Next morning, staring at the pieces, turning the futile twisted hands of the clock in my hands, I realised that all I had done was the merest repetition. Hadn't my mother, our dear dead father's relict, long ago done just the same thing in front of me at Southwell? She had; and I was choked with fresh fury at the thought. That day, determined that there must be some deed which would break me from the spiral that is Time, I drew up my will. In it, my dear sister, I left you all that I possess. A just exchange, as Philip Sidney would have said, since *you*, my Augusta, are all that I want to possess.

The last month of her pregnancy, Belle went, I think, in terror for her life. She thought I was mad (so I was, Guss, but only for you), so what should she do but write and invite you to come again and stay at Piccadilly Terrace, to attend her until her confinement, and during it. You came, you saw me sitting staring at the squat ruby bottle, and you took the liberty of uttering the word *duty* in my earshot. You must have thought I was very drugged indeed. I told you to leave duty to God. It occurs to me now that you may have felt it was your 'duty' to present yourself at that point as a sort of barrier between myself and Annabella. I hope not.

On Sunday the 10th of December, Belle gave birth, and I had another daughter, to which you were midwife. I insisted upon the names with which she was christened: Augusta Ada. Just over a month later, as you know, Lady Byron took the child and left me, ostensibly at first to join her parents in Leicestershire, at Kirkby Mallory, but I believe that from the moment she walked out through the door it was never her intention to live with me again. During the month of March of that year of 1816, Newstead Abbey was shaken by a small earthquake, and staining the page with my tears I wrote the first draft of a perfectly disgusting little poem to my dear departed wife:

Fare thee well! And if for ever,
Still for ever, fare thee well:
Even though unforgiving, never
Gainst thee shall my heart rebel. . . .

I don't quite know what inspired me to tell so many lies in making such sweet music of Belle's going. Before long, I had lies enough back in return, with Lady Byron's legal advisers putting it out that I was mad, that I had tried to murder her by firing at her with a pistol while she lay in bed carrying my child, that I secretly indulged in obscene literature (by which she meant that I kept a

(X X X)

copy of Sade's *Justine* in a drawer in my desk), oh and all the dismal rest of it too dreary for recall. . . .

None of this, I confess, gave me very great grounds for alarm. But it was a little different, my dear Guss, to hear from the lips of the admirable Hobhouse one fine morning towards the end of that same month of March that I was done for unless I signed a deed of separation and left England for ever and at once. I stared at him in horror and disbelief. 'Hobby!' I cried. 'How so?'

Then I was informed that Lady Byron had instructed her advocates Dr Stephen Lushington and Sir Samuel Romilly in the secrets of the marriage bed. They were to accuse me of a criminal taste for the vice of sodomy, a capital offence under English law, should I not amicably agree to my wife's terms concerning legal and financial arrangements. This was Luciferian enough, I suppose, especially as Annabella had plainly omitted to tell her lawyers of her own delight in this particular form of intimacy, with a consequence that she appeared now in the rôle of the abused party; but Hobhouse added to the general horror of that moment even before I had a chance to respond to the first charge.

'Lady Byron,' he whispered, 'intends also to accuse you of worse.'

'What worse?' I said.

'Of incest with your sister,' Hobhouse said.

I felt, I confess, as if he had struck me in the face; even more appallingly, Augusta, it was as if he had struck *you*. . . . 'My dear friend,' I said, 'are you sure of this?'

'As sure as I am that you will be ruined if it ever comes to court,' Hobhouse answered.

'But how could she hope to prove such a thing?' I demanded.

'For God's sake!' Hobhouse cried. 'Lady Byron has told her lawyers that you were forever in Mrs Leigh's company from the moment of your marriage; that you said you preferred Mrs Leigh to her; that you left your bed in this very house and went to your sister's bed and that she heard the two of you laughing together.'

'*Laughing?*' I said.

'Laughing,' repeated Hobby in the gravest of tones.

'The devil,' I said, 'if we haven't discovered a new perversion. I never knew that laughing could be construed as a sexual act.'

But Hobhouse refused to join in my bluff. He was pulling his nose with the thumb and forefinger of his right hand, and shaking his head as if to rid it of some buzzing hurt, and generally looking for the road to Samarkand in the pattern of my Persian carpet. In short, he was embarrassed beyond words – a condition probably novel to a man of his suavity. 'My dear Byron,' he managed at last, in a low choking voice, 'is any of it true?'

'Is any of what true?' I said.

'What your wife accuses you of,' he said.

'Laughing with my sister,' I said.

He got up then and went and stood at the sun-lit window with his broad back to me. There was a long silence, during which I drank one of my bottles of soda water and sought by staring at them to compel my hands to stop their trembling, though within my breast I believe my heart was behaving like a volcano.

'Then it *is* true,' Hobhouse said, at last, without

turning to look upon me. He sighed. 'You'd better know also,' he went on, 'that your wife has letters from Lady Caroline Lamb, letters in which she swears that you often boasted to her of things you had done to young boys –'

'I should have killed that silly bitch,' I said.

'Yes,' Hobby said. 'You'd have done better to have murdered her. There are judges who reckon sodomy worse than murder.'

In vain I protested to him that it was all a dirty plot, a sort of blackmail, by means of which Lady Byron and her lawyers were seeking to frighten me into granting her a separation on her terms. But my friend insisted that matters were far more serious and specific. Sodomy, he kept saying, was a gallows crime, and besides had I not considered how the imputation of incest would corrupt and dishonour the name of my sister for ever? Did I not realise that half London was already ablaze with the vile rumours of my depravity, and that my enemies wanted nothing more keenly than that I should attempt to defend myself in court, to drag me down and disgrace me and destroy me? Perhaps unbeknownst to myself, Hobhouse said, I had made enemies in the very highest places, among powerful persons who detested both my poetry and my politics. These people would lose no time in making a martyr of my wife and a monster of me, nor would they have much difficulty in doing so once they had succeeded in lashing the great British public into one of its periodic fits of morality.

When Hobhouse finally turned round from the window I swear that I saw bright tears in his eyes. 'My dear Byron,' he said, 'I beg you to be prudent, to listen for once to reason. Grant Lady Byron this separation she is asking for. It is my opinion that your wretched marriage means nothing to you, anyway. Agree to her terms. Do not defend the case. Go abroad.'

I stared into his broad round face and saw my fate there. I was now to *be* the hero I had so often celebrated in my verses: not so much a Childe Harold as a Cain or a Manfred, an outcast from my own kind, a wanderer in foreign lands, gloomily absorbed in the memory of my past sins and the injustices done me by society, a soul in outer darkness howling dismally. I think I smiled.

I said, 'Just give me one real unanswerable reason why I should go.'

'For your sister's sake,' said Hobby.

So I went, my dearest Augusta. I think, to be sure, that I would have shot myself, had I not been too conscious of the pleasure such an event would have given to my mother-in-law. However, if I could have been sure of an even ghostly after-life in which it was permitted to me to haunt the old bitch, I would most willingly have pulled the trigger. But as second prize to death, I chose imperfect exile, my father's way. And now I am convinced that my bones will never rest in an English grave, nor my clay mix with the earth of that country. I believe the thought might drive me mad on my death-bed, could I suppose that any of my friends would be cruel or base enough to convey my carcase back. England, I will not even feed your worms, if I can help it.

Nothing of interest happened today, so I have lived only in these sad, bad, beautiful, and terrible memories of the past. Now I must snuff out the flame and try to sleep. I wish, oh how I wish, Augusta, dearest, that you could sleep beside me, but I have to accept that the probability is that I shall never see again your beloved face, like an infinite improvement on my own, neither in my bed nor out of it. Alas, poor human nature! Good night, or rather, morning. It is four, and the dawn gleams over the Grand Canal, and unshadows the Rialto.

CHAPTER FOURTEEN

I Go into Exile, and Meet Shelley

This book being for the most part (though with the regrettable exception of the last chapter) *memoranda* rather than confessions, it is not my intention to note in detail the various places through which I now passed, any more than it was in the case of my first pilgrimage.

For, be it said at the outset, I immediately became Childe Harold again, and this time with a freer and franker assumption of that peculiar character than heretofore I would have believed possible. England had flung me from her shores, more or less, and my departure was now not for a voyage, but a banishment. I went forth sad and angered as Adam from paradise. When your native land believes you to be incompatible with her repose, and there is no choice left you but to abandon her, then you must act as swiftly and cleanly as you can, though in so doing you forsake perhaps a half of your existence. Exile is a mortal malady of the heart; yet it is also the human condition.

On the 21st of April 1816, I signed the deed of separation from Lady Byron and turned my back on the cureless wound of our marriage. Four days later I crossed from Dover on the Channel packet, taking with me into exile a small folding writing-desk, a dozen pairs of nankeen breeches, and a splendid coach made to my specifications by Baxter. This coach, modelled upon Napoleon's, cost me £500, and required six horses to pull it. Hobhouse and Scrope accompanied me to the coast. That last evening in England I remember I went with my friends to visit the tomb of the poet Charles Churchill in the graveyard at Dover. I lay down upon the grave and then I gave the sexton a crown to fresh turf it. The packet sailed next morning a little after nine. The bustle kept me in spirits, but as the boat stood out I found myself affected and pulled off my cap and waved it to Hobby and Scrope where they were watching on the quay.

Fare thee well! Thus disunited,
Torn from every nearer tie,
Sear'd in heart, and lone, and blighted
More than this I scarce can die.

The lines I had lyingly addressed to Annabella came back to haunt me with their truth as I observed the white cliffs melt into the mist. It was not a happy crossing. But by the time we reached Ostend I was sufficiently revived in body and soul to fall like a thunderbolt upon the chambermaid.

After passing through Bruges and Ghent and Antwerp, we were detained for some days in dreary Brussels, it being necessary to effect some repairs to my carriage. I took advantage of this enforced delay, by visiting the battlefield at Waterloo. The reader interested in my thoughts on regarding this fate-fraught field will find them in the third canto of *Childe Harold*, written with my habitual rapidity at this time. From there we rolled on in splendour to Switzerland by way of the Meuse and Rhine valleys, my health and spirits gradually improving as we came in sight of the mountains. The gentians were in bloom when we rode through the Jura and came to Sécheron, near Geneva, where on the 25th of May we put up at the Hotel Angleterre. In the hotel register I wrote down my age as 100. Then my attention was caught by a name and a title just above mine on the same page of the register: *Percy Bysshe Shelley*, it said, and then (with a nice flourish) *Atheist*.

I will admit that my heart sank at first, and also that my initial impressions of the poet Shelley were not exactly favourable. In this, I was in part influenced by the fact that he had journeyed to Sécheron a few days earlier, accompanied by his wife Mary and her sister Claire, not just in order to meet me, but so that Claire might announce to me the decidedly unwelcome news that she was pregnant with my child. In the depths of my confusion in London, following the departure of Annabella and my enforced separation from Augusta while threats of divorce and worse were flying to and fro, this odious young creature had sailed into my life under the pretext that she was writing a novel, about which she required my opinion. In no time at all, she had invited me to take her into the country for a night of passion. That is what she called it, adding that she adored me, and wanted nothing better than to make me briefly happy. As to that night, the truth is that for me it helped to pass time which might otherwise have been worse. But here was Claire Clairmont pregnant as a consequence, and travelled some eight hundred miles to give me the good news. Nor did she clap her plump hands at my suggestion that she might consider an abortion. She was in love with the idea of being loved by the poet Byron; now she had added to this the blessed idea of being mother to the poet Byron's child.

I did my best to concentrate what remained of my Claire-shocked wits on the poet Shelley. At first glance, or second, he had his points of resemblance to a beautiful but ineffectual angel, but once the ear grew used to his strident voice and the mind accepted the singular purity of his enthusiasms then it was impossible not to recognise that he possessed or was possessed by a genius not at all removed from reality. I had read his *Queen Mab*, and quite admired it, but his conversation, once his shyness evaporated, revealed that the poetry he had written up to that point reflected only a fraction of the sublime glitter of his mind. A lover of ideas, he proved the most entrancing and engrossing conversationalist. I found my spirit quickened by contact with him, and we discovered key literary tastes in common, though I never could understand what he saw in the amiable but idiotic Wordsworth, and for his part he refused to admit the music of the little nightingale of Twickenham. When I rented the Villa Diodati, just above the Maison Chappius, where Milton had once stayed, we spent much time together, walking and talking, rowing and sailing on the lake. Shelley had taken a house which lay on the other side of the vineyards. With his wife Mary, and the ineluctable Claire, we tried our hands at composing ghost stories, though only Mary persevered in the attempt, writing a fine piece of nonsense about the monster created by a Dr Victor Frankenstein (in which I always thought that the doctor bore a distinct resemblance to her husband, and the monster to me). We made a tour by boat of the Lake of Geneva, visiting the Castle of Chillon and Gibbon's decayed summer-house at Lausanne where he finished his *History*. At the latter place I gathered some acacia leaves from the terrace to preserve in remembrance both of Gibbon and of my being there with Shelley, for I was already convinced of my new friend's immortality. Truth to tell, I preferred sailing with Shelley to walking with him, since he had a long loping stride and was always forging on ahead with the two women while I limped behind. On water, we were equals. The drift of his mind, ever reaching upwards for the ungraspable, was just about the opposite of mine, yet there was an undercurrent or depth of harmony in existence between the two of us. I think it is only right to set it on record that in my opinion he is far more intelligent than I am, and capable of a concentration and a power of coherent thought beside which I must appear the merest intellectual butterfly. Yet whether Shelley, for all his brilliance, has ever understood me, or penetrated to my essential nature, I beg leave to doubt. We could gossip and converse with the spontaneity of quicksilver, yet our hearts remained strangers to each other. All the same, I love him more than any man I ever met, unselfishly; and it is a love the stronger and more durable for having no fleshliness in it.

I called him Shiloh, he called me Albé. My nickname came about because one evening when the four of us were out in the boat together, the wind stirred up the waves, and I grew excited and promised to sing them an Albanian song. 'Listen!' I cried. 'Be sentimental!

Lend me your ears!' Then I stood up in the bows of the boat, threw back my head, and let forth a long wild howl like a wolf's. The women were disappointed, having anticipated some oriental yodelling, but I declared to my captive audience that what they had just heard was an exact imitation of the mode of the inhabitants of the mountains of Albania. (And so it was, though it would have been Greek to my wife.) From that day, all three of them called me Albé, and Shelley himself (as when he came here to Venice last summer about the Allegra affair) likes to throw back his head on first greeting me with the nickname, and howl like a wolf.

Incidentally, remembrance of my time with Shelley when in buzzing about Lake Geneva we found ourselves following the footsteps of Rousseau, brings it also back to my mind to say something on the subject of that little French philosopher, since I have been compared with him often enough. My mother, before I was twenty, would have it that I was like Rousseau, and Madame de Staël used to say so too, and the *Edinburgh Review* has something of the sort in its critique of the fourth canto of *Childe Harold*. Yet for the life of me, I can't see any real point of resemblance. Rousseau wrote prose, I verse; he was of the people, I am of the aristocracy; he was a philosopher, I am none; he published his first work at forty, I mine at eighteen; his first essay brought him universal applause, mine the contrary; he married his housekeeper, I could not keep house with my wife; he thought all the world in a plot against *him*, my little world seems to think *me* in a plot against it, if I may judge by the abuse in print and coterie; he liked botany, I like flowers, and herbs, and trees, but know nothing of their pedigrees; he wrote music, I limit my knowledge of it to what I catch by *ear* (I never could learn anything by study, not even a language, it was all by rote and ear and memory); he had a bad memory, I *had* at least an excellent one until here in Venice these last two years I began to muddy it with women; he wrote with hesitation and care, I with rapidity and rarely with pains; *he* could never ride nor swim, nor was 'cunning of fence', *I* am an excellent swimmer, a decent though not at all a dashing rider (having staved in a rib at eighteen in the course of scampering), and am sufficient of fence, particularly of the Highland broad-sword.... Consider, can you imagine Rousseau as a prizefighter? Yet I am not at all a bad boxer when I can keep my temper, which is difficult, but which I have striven to do ever since I knocked down my sparring partner, a Mr Purling, and put his knee-pan out (with the gloves on) in Angelo's and Jackson's rooms back in 1806. Besides, Rousseau's way of life, his country, his manners, his whole character, were so very different, that I am at a loss to conceive how such a comparison could have arisen, as it has done three several times, and all in rather a remarkable manner. I forgot to say that *he* was also famously short-sighted, and that hitherto my eyes have been the contrary to such a degree that in the largest theatre of Bologna I distinguished and read some busts and inscriptions painted near the stage, from a box so distant, and so darkly lighted, that none of the company (composed of young and very bright-eyed people, some of them in the same box) could make out a letter, and thought it was a trick, though I had never been in that theatre before. Altogether, I think myself justified in thinking the comparison not well-founded. I don't say this out of pique, for Rousseau was a great man, and the thing if true were flattering enough. But I never cared to be pleased with a chimera.

The Shelleys, along with Claire, left Switzerland for England; Hobby and Scrope Davies came to Coligny and we decided to drive to Venice, journeying down through the Simplon Pass in my Napoleonic coach. In Milan I stopped off to visit the Ambrosian Library and inspect some autograph letters of Lucrezia Borgia; along with the letters, I was allowed to see and fondle a long lock of Lucrezia's bright yellow hair, and it was no great trick to contrive to wind a single strand of this hair about my wrist while the curator's attention was distracted by a living woman coming down the stairs. I wear that bracelet still as I write these words. When I die they can bury it with me, so that if ever my tomb is disturbed (as in the verses by John Donne) the finders of my skeleton may suppose that the hair once belonged to my love. In Verona I stopped off also, to visit the amphitheatre and Juliet's tomb. It was the middle of November, most negative of months in any clime, when at last we came to Venice.

Venice, from the start, pleased me as much as I had expected it would, and I had expected much. It is one of those places which I seem to have known even before I ever saw them, and after the East I think the idea of it always haunted my mind. I like the gloomy gaiety of the gondolas, and the silence of the canals. Probably this place is the greenest island of my imagination. I do not even regret the evident decay of the city. I have been familiar with ruins too long to dislike desolation.

I like the Venetian dialect, and the pink marbles of the Palazzi, and the cafés on the Square of St Mark's, but these are things which everyone likes, are they not? I like also the stink of the canals when the mist rises from them at nightfall, and the painted and pox-patched whores, female and male, who kneel down or bend over for the instant pleasure of their clients even in broad daylight in the alleys near the Campo San Angelo. It is hard to be bored with oneself in Venice, and for that I am grateful. The slow fever of the place keeps even my stagnant heart alive.

That first Carnival here, however, brought me low and into half-delirium as a result of late nights and dissipations. It was in this condition that I learned in a letter from Shelley that Claire had given birth, in Bath, to my daughter Allegra. A letter from the mother followed hot. I responded by promising my support just so long as I never had to look at the dam again. In this, if I appear hard-hearted, or without any heart at all, so be it. The reader, I take it, will not have had to *listen* to Miss Clairmont in full flood. The lady is pleasantly and promiscuously vicious, where my wife might be said to be a virtuous monster, but otherwise they have a lot in common.

My lodgings that first winter here were in the Frezzeria, near San Marco, with a draper called Segati, whose young wife Marianna supplied all my needs, sometimes as often as three times a day. I completed my blank verse drama *Manfred* in these agreeable circumstances, and bought a complete set of the works of Voltaire in 92 volumes, and even started reading them.

CHAPTER FIFTEEN

I Go to Rome, and Witness an Execution

I HAVE BEEN dreaming today of taking Allegra away from the Hoppners, and skipping off to Venezuela, and starting a new life in that incomparably free and enlightened country. The money from the sale of Newstead has been paid into my bank, and I have sent my instructions to Murray that *Don Juan* is to be published without omissions or any alterings. Just yesterday I wrote also to Augusta telling her that I have never ceased to love her, and indeed that I am utterly incapable of *real* love for any other human being. This declaration is true, the sober truth, and yet here, privately – (and I fear it *is* private since surely that chapter in which I confessed my feelings for my sister must ensure that these *Memoirs* can never be published in the lifetime of either of us) – privately, and for the ease of my own heart, though it hurts me more to say so than anything I have yet said, I must also remark that it seems to me now that Augusta's love for me has been somehow *frozen*, who knows how, though I suspect the dread influence (like a moral influenza) of Lady Byron somewhere in this process. But Venezuela beckons.... About which country I know nothing, which of course is why I desire to go there, to be free of my countess from Ravenna, and my past, and this wretched identity in which I can no longer take pleasure, or pain, or anything at all.

Tom Moore is here. I gave him some of these papers, with the proviso that I am withholding certain chapters from his eyes, and that in any case the whole is unfinished, seeing that I have not yet quite brought the general story of my days up to the present moment. The fact that Moore will not be reading the chapter to hand, at least until after my death, and perhaps not even then, gives me the chance to set it on record now that I have never quite made up my mind as to whether I like Moore or not. He is charming all right, but his charm is like that Parisian oil which he employs to dress his hair, slightly scented and vulgar. He has talent in his verses, but then talent is not enough, and that is *all* his verses have. He is a little dandy, to be sure, but it seems to me that after a certain age it is a criticism of a man if he remains dandified. At Moore's age and stage, one ought at least to be a *ruined* dandy. After our dinner last night I took him through the canals in my gondola to see Venice by moonlight. He had nothing to say about it which did not grate upon my ears as a pretty platitude. At the end of our circuit, as we came gliding under the Rialto, he started to sing one of his Irish songs as if he considered that an adequate response to the beauty and the horror of the night. I heard him out until we reached the Vendramin. Then I threw back my head and gave him a blast of Albania.

While I was masking two years ago at the time of that first of my Carnivals, Hobhouse had gone on importunately to Rome. Venice was not to my sober friend's taste. He disapproved, I believe, of my relish in this city of garlic sauce and Desdemona, of quays and masks and fireworks and guitars and bastard Latin. Rome, he declared, was a far more serious place. And so it was, and so I let him go there.

That spring, though, Hobby summoned me to join him. Recovering from my fevers, being nursed by the admirable Marianna, I was reluctant to move, but in the end I went. Not, however, before, sitting up in bed at my landlord's, the draper's, and eating a bowl of cherries popped into my mouth by his wife, my mistress, I wrote in about fifteen minutes what I still consider one of my finest and least affected poems:

So we'll go no more a-roving
So late into the night,
Though the heart be still as loving,
And the moon be still as bright.
For the sword outwears its sheath,
And the soul wears out the breast,
And the heart must pause to breathe,
And Love itself have rest.
Though the night was made for loving,
And the day returns too soon,
Yet we'll go no more a-roving
By the light of the moon.

By which I meant, I daresay, that I was now twenty-nine years old, and beginning to wonder if it would be altogether wise to spend the rest of my life tooling and fooling. On the way to one assignation just before this, as it happens, I had slipped while getting into my gondola and fallen into the Grand Canal, and there is nothing like a mouthful of Venetian shit to bring a man to his senses. All the same, I make myself sound far too reasonable, and I have to admit that at the instant of writing (3 a.m., Tuesday the 18th of May, 1819) there is no more sign of my sword having outworn its sheath than there is of my soul having saved itself. What I earn by my brains, I spend on my ballocks, and there's an end of it.

On the road to Rome, I passed close to Lake Trasimene, which I knew from my childhood when the minister Paterson used to like to describe to me the ground there all covered with corpses, and the swift stream running scarlet with the blood of Romans and Carthaginians – a prospect which had played its part in awakening my own interest in history. Now the local peasantry showed me that stream, which is still named the Sanguinetto. The lake itself was like a sheet of silver. I liked it there.

Rome I did not like. Hobby did his best, dragging me along from one holy or unholy site to another. I find that I have nothing to say about any of them; it is all quite indescribable in any case, and the guide-book fails as honourably as anything. I saw the Apollo Belvedere: it was the image of Lady Adelaide Forbes, whom Moore once proposed to me as a possible bride; I think I never saw such a good likeness. I saw the Pope alive, and a cardinal dead, both of whom looked very well indeed. (The latter was in state in the Chiesa Nuova, previous to his interment.) By the by, in this matter of touristic visitations, descriptions of art and architecture, and so forth, I have more than once reflected to myself that sensibility needs to be well-laced with humour in verbal responses to such things, lest the human spark be lost. There is nothing much worse, or more depressing, than unleavened sensibility. *Childe Harold* could do with some jokes.

The Forum, the Pantheon, St Peter's, the Colosseum – all Rome struck me as a necropolis. There is a sweet and sickly smell of death even on the Spanish Steps and up on the Palatine. Rome is beautiful no doubt, but its beauty is the beauty of a corpse.

One night in the Piazza di Spagna, on my way back from the opera, I saw something a little more interesting than the Arch of Septimus Severus. A fine, well-made lad of seventeen or eighteen summers was standing naked before a small group of sympathetic and attentive spectators. As I drew nearer, I saw that his member was standing up stiff before his belly in the torchlight, throbbing with desire and expectation. He was a pleasant enough fellow, respectful and well-mannered, you might say, but in that corner of the buildings, sheltered by the outspread cloaks of the onlookers, there he was consumed with lust, nevertheless. Up stepped a kindly, sympathetic, slightly older man, and as I watched this second performer gently inserted into the eye of the erect penis three or four tiny candles of the sort used to celebrate a child's birthday. The older man then proceeded to light these candles, and the little flames thus brought into being served to show up the contours of the young boy's belly – of his whole torso – in beautiful relief. The boy's penis was now throbbing and jerking in excitement, and each time it did so the lights and shadows on his body flickered and danced, with this detail and that first revealed and then obscured. It was incredibly and excruciatingly tantalising, both to the spectators and, as I had to believe, to the boy himself. But presently the wax from the candles began to drip, all hot and molten. And as the first drops touched the boy's penis the pain was at once so dreadful and so exciting that – unable to help or stop himself – he began to come. This the boy did with such force that the tiny candles were carried up with the jets of it, and tumbled about in the air, casting lights upon his body more dancing and ephemeral than ever. He had in front of him a veritable fountain of little spots of fire. Then, having gone up, the blobs and flecks of flame came cascading down – over his genitalia, down his thighs, down his knees and his calves, to be extinguished in the dirt at his feet. Some of the spectators seemed to grow quite mad and enflamed with the spectacle, and I noted more than one of them jacking himself off secretly in the shadows as he watched. But what struck me most was that the boy's *face* never showed any desire, any sign of excitement or satisfaction, at all; it was a veritable white mask, cold and expressionless, in the small circle of brightly flickering torches. When he had finished, there was no applause, and he was gone into the darkness almost before you could blink, while the older man passed through the crowd with his hat, and gold and silver coins were tossed in it. I learned later, in a brothel near the Quirinal, that the boy in question would have been some sort of itinerant semi-professional, and that his act has the name of 'Firecrackers à la Mode de Firenza'.

The other thing I saw in Rome, and which has remained with me since in my dreams, happened on the day before I left the eternal city. Accompanied by Hobhouse, and wearing my best biscuit-coloured breeches, I went along to a public execution. Three thieves were to be beheaded in the middle of a piazza. I took my seat in the shade of a balcony. The procession came into the square, led by priests in white masks, who were followed by a pair of half-naked executioners. Then came the three criminals, heavily manacled, hobbling along behind a perfectly hideous crucifix and a billowing black banner with Christ upon it. Soldiers with muskets surrounded the scaffold and the thieves approached the block. The first of the victims made a great fuss of dying. He kept screaming and kicking as they forced him to bend down. He was a huge fellow, as fat as the Prince Regent, and the hole in the head-block was too narrow for his neck, so they had to pommel and pound and squeeze until he would fit. The axe flashed and fell. His body jumped like a Punchinello. The head rolled from the block with its mouth still gaping open in a shout, and the blood came shooting from his neck like the spout of a whale. The sight turned me quite hot and thirsty, making me shake so that I could hardly hold my opera-glass between my fingers. (I was close, but was determined to see, as one should see everything once, with attention.) No doubt it is odd, but I can scarcely remember the second and third executions. The first, perhaps, had blunted the edge of my sensibilities.

Is this so very surprising? I think not. The spectacle of such horrors is terrible, but familiarity can breed contempt even for violent death. That first beheading I watched with fascination, the second with distaste, and the third with an indifference which was almost boredom. I rose from my chair and I wiped the beads of perspiration from my forehead and my upper lip. Of course, I would have saved the three men if I could.

I detested Rome. It was with a sigh of relief that I stepped into my carriage and headed for the cool, clean air of the Apennines. Returned to Venice, I found letters from Augusta waiting for me. These letters were full of woes, as usual, megrims and mysteries; but my sympathies remained in suspense, since for the life of me I couldn't make out whether her disorder was a broken heart or an ear-ache brought on by listening to Lady Byron.

One final memory of my time in Rome. On the roof of St Peter's I encountered an English family: father, mother, daughter, seeing the sights. As I approached them, I realised that I'd been recognised. The father's face changed colour and his elbow went into his wife. The wife then turned swiftly to the daughter and snapped open her parasol to shield her. 'That is Lord Byron!' I heard her say in a loud whisper. 'Avert your eyes, dear! He is dangerous to look at!'

CHAPTER SIXTEEN

I Come to the Palazzo Mocenigo, and Write this Book

I KNEW A MAN (Lord G) who died of an inflammation of the bowels: so they took them out, and sent them (on account of their discrepancies), separately from the carcass, to England. Conceive a man going one way, and his intestines another, and his immortal soul a third! Was there ever such a distribution? One certainly has a soul; but how it came to allow itself to be enclosed in a body is more than I can imagine. I only know if once mine gets out, I'll have a bit of a tussle before I let it get in again. Pardon my digression.

Venetians, being wise, and disdaining fevers, are not in the habit of summering in their city. I leased a large country house, the Villa Foscarini, on the left bank of the Brenta, near La Mira, a village about seven miles inland from the river's mouth at Fusina on the lagoon. Here I sat under the olives in my garden and laboured on the fourth canto of *Childe Harold*, then suddenly threw that aside to blaze into a new poem, *Beppo*, a nice enough tissue of digressions upon everything from fish sauce to Shakespeare, all based on a stupid anecdote I heard from Marianna's husband, the cuckold draper. The mock-heroics of *Beppo*, and the way I deliberately ignored the 'Byronic' possibilities of that chap's wanderings and adventures in favour of a scene over a cup of coffee – this, though I say it myself, marks something new in my verse, and the verse of my time. I was tired to death of writing more Harold stuff, of all that pilgrimage of philosophical pretentiousness and the style like that of a great soul going through life on stilts. I liked the snap and the bite of the voice I discovered then. The tone of it harks back to Pope and to Juvenal, the writers I really admire, as well as to the light-heartedness of the *commedia dell'arte* and the spirit of the novels of Sterne and of Rabelais. Writing *Beppo* was for me the beginning of me.

Murray, it need hardly be said, did not care for the change in my style. But then Murray had complained about *Manfred* as well, saying it was blasphemous and obscene and the Lord knows what, and regretting that he had ever published such a wicked work, and this while all the time the copies were selling quicker than he could print them. My answer to such literary criticism was to demand of him the sum of £2500 for the fourth slice of Harold; which money he paid, though moaning and groaning like a half-broken virgin, and pretending to be scandalised by my mercenary conversion. Yet, in truth, I can't think my price was too high. Moore, after all, got £3000 out of Longman for his latest effort, *Lalla Rookh*, a box of Turkish delights with the sugar mostly stolen from me. What do such as Tom Moore pay *for* their verses? A sentimental tear or two; a passing sigh. Whereas my living-costs in Venice have been about £5000 in the last couple of years, more than half of which has been spent on women, i.e. in the active service of the Muse, Erato.

That summer and autumn which I spent upon the Brenta was punctuated also by a series of wheedling, silly letters from the most regrettable Claire. I should never have gone to bed with that creature, but there it is. I had never professed to care for her, yet she couldn't accept this. In the rarefied atmosphere of the Shelley circle, any sexual union, however brief, is invariably exalted into some glorious fluttering fusion of souls. It was in these terms – like one angel cooing to another across a luminous void – that my bright friend's dowdy little sister-in-law now began non-stop to write to me. Having equipped herself with all the maternal stops, she was determined to pull them out without restraint. Addressing me, after an eighteen months' silence on my part, as 'My dearest friend', she treated me to an elaborate description of Allegra's features, complete with poetical touches such as that the poor infant had 'eyes of a dazzling blue more like the waters of the lake of Geneva under a summer sky than anything else I ever saw, rosy projecting lips, and a little square chin dented in the middle exactly like your own'. She sent me a lock of Allegra's hair, and a lot of other stuff in which to be frank she *used* our daughter in a blatant and self-pitying attempt to worm her own way back into my life. As letter followed letter, and each more scented and shrieking and maladroit than the last, I hardened towards her until I had reached a position of immovable distaste. I vowed then that I would never meet Claire Clairmont again, and I never have; yet before I am condemned out of hand for my cruelty or my levity in the matter, let it be put in the balance that to Allegra herself I have proved a benevolent father, and that it is my intention to see her well educated and furnished with a handsome dowry in due course. It worries me presently that the child might not be happy with the Hoppners. Hoppner himself is a sound enough fellow, if obsequious, but his wife is a straitlaced Switzer matron. I keep coming back to the idea that Allegra might be best placed in a convent where she could be taught to practise a religion, and believe. But perhaps in this I am guilty of trying to turn my bastard daughter into my own soul, and wish on her the fate which Scott said would be mine? Shelley, when he was here with me last August, said no less as we rode down the Lido.

Shelley: he is surely a mixture without parallel of physical contrasts and harmonies. I have heard that in his adolescence he was considered good-looking – but now he is no longer truly so. His features are delicate, but not regular, except for his mouth, which however is not good when he laughs, and is in any case more than a little spoiled by his teeth, the shape of them being not in keeping with his refinement. His features, in short, remind me of a whippet's. Once upon a time, one can still see, his skin must have been white and fine; though ever since I have known him it has been covered with freckles, either from exposure to rough weather or by reason of his health. Let's see, what else? An extremely small head, hands, and feet. Hair, chestnut-coloured and thick but not well-groomed, already invaded by some premature silver threads. He is very tall, but so bent that he seems of ordinary stature, and although very slight in his whole person, his bones and his joints are prominent and even coarse. And yet all these elements opposed to beauty form an exceedingly sympathetic being – and I must stress the word Being, for truly my friend Shelley is rather a Spirit than a man. He is also extraordinary in his garb, for he normally wears a jacket like a young college boy's, never any gloves, nor polish on his boots – and yet set him down in a crowd in London or Rome, of the most polished society, and it is Shelley who will stand out as the most finished of gentlemen. His voice, as I have remarked, is shrill, even strident; nevertheless, it is modulated by the drift of his thoughts, and has a grace, a gentleness, a delicacy that goes straight to the heart. I think, in short, that I never knew a person of either sex so deficient in beauty who still can produce such an impression of it by their presence. It is the fire of Shelley's genius that transforms his features.

The rains began; the leaves of autumn drifted down the Brenta; in November 1817, my lease of the Villa Foscarini being nearly expired, I took a golden-prowed gondola back to Venice. There, that December, I heard the good news from Spooney: the Newstead estate had been sold at last to Tom Wildman, whom I had known at Harrow when he was covered with boils and never had a sixpence to his name. With such a prospect of funds opening up before me, I rented until further notice at £200 per annum this sumptuous rotting residence where I still sit scribbling, my Palazzo Mocenigo on the Grand Canal. Hobhouse joined me for Christmas – I remember we jawed of Hume all Christmas Eve, which bruised my brains and left me feeling quite jaundiced. Always the vulture for culture, my old friend succeeded also in dragging me behind him to La Fenice, our Venetian opera-house, where we saw Rossini's *Othello* and the *Don Giovanni* of Amadeus Mozart. (Both works I admire, though I find them too close to home for comfort.) Having rid myself of Marianna Segati for a bed-warmer, I entered then a world of other harlotry, caught the clap from a lady called Elena da Mosta, and cured myself by swimming from the Lido to the end of the Grand Canal. This last achievement came in my winning a swimming contest. I competed against two of my friends – Angelo Mangaldo and Alexander Scott – and I won by three quarters of a mile, after being continuously in the water for three and three quarter hours.

That spring Allegra came to live with me: a new flame in the gloom of my heart, a fresh and bright-eyed spirit in my house. She ran upstairs and down like a sweet little devil in a snood, shrieking for puppets and sherbet powders, upsetting my library, getting marmalade on the Dante, spilling milk all over the papers of a poem just begun (*Mazeppa*, its name). I loved my darling bastard from the moment I first set eyes on her. (Damn Shelley for being right, that this is no fit place for her to live!) Feeling whimsical tonight, I might even entertain the notion that it was under the dear demon Allegra's influence that I began *Don Juan* and the present writing. Her innocent heart made me want to make sense of my life. But now I am drivelling on like Wordsworthless, the Lord of the Lakers himself, and having reached the point in my narrative where I started the actual penning of it, perhaps it is time for me to stop, before I lose my way in baa-baa bleatings, intimations of immortality, all that. . . .

Impressed or depressed, I suppose, by the variableness of my moods, both Shelley and my new mistress the Countess Guiccioli, on separate occasions and under different provocations, have seen fit to liken me to the chameleon. I must protest against this simile, and I shall now give my reason, trusting that by this act the reader will pardon me the necessity of any further summation of my own soul or character. The chameleon, as I understand, takes protectively the colour of its surroundings. When in all my days did I ever do that? I take not their colour on myself to hide myself, but *from* their colour all I need to display myself.

It is dawn, and I am tired. Ho-hum. Byron, good night. Good night, Allegra.

CHAPTER SEVENTEEN

A Postscript: 22nd April, 1822

Good night, Allegra. . . . I wrote those words nearly three years ago, and thought that I was done with my little self-history. I had reached, as I said, that moment in my narrative where I had begun the writing of it. Most of the chapters were given to Moore, although I kept a copy of the whole. I imagined, or convinced myself, at all events, not that my life was done, but that my story-telling about it was at an end. A neat enough packet, I thought, though probably unpublishable in the way, and for the good reasons, that the truth always is. When – on Tuesday, the first of June, 1810 – I left Venice in order to follow Teresa to Ravenna, I sealed up the papers, and expected not to open such matters again.

Now those seals are undone. I am in Pisa. I have the saddest addition to make to my story. Let me put off the writing of that, though, the news which I just learned the day before yesterday, and which might well break my heart – had I any such organ of luxury left in my frame – if I do not rein in the passions, compelling myself as author to a certain verisimilitude, a cold regard for the pageant of events, a respecting of chronology. I must not blurt out what I have to say, though that is my natural way, and I may choke in denying it.

I had only planned to visit Teresa for a month. As it happened, I stayed three, our affair prospering despite the fact that I found her there in her palazzo at Ravenna quite ill, with a consumption feared. I loved Teresa and nursed her, settling into the rôle of a *cavaliere servente*, chatting over herbal tea, riding with her in her carriage through the pine forests, watched all the while by her crafty and benevolent husband, the ancient Count himself. My love for Teresa, I might claim, involved me in perils and escapes, at this time, besides which those of my hero Don Juan might be reckoned the merest child's play. The key to my love for this faithful and foolhardy lady is perhaps that she could share in my laughter at all such scrapes and mishaps; I never knew another grown woman with whom I could laugh so, excepting my sister. Yet Teresa was serious, too, and when I showed her the ring in which I had secreted a tiny phial of poison, promising that I would kill myself if she died of her sickness, she shocked me by retorting that I should provide just another such ring for her use, since she could not conceive of any more life without me. Leaving logic on one side, this mightily impressed me. For the first time since that winter with Augusta I was sure that somebody loved me, and not for my name or my fame, but because I am nobody else.

The summer waxed. The heat in Ravenna grew intolerable. I lived in a frowsty hotel, at the mercy of the Count. He knew, of course, that the English milord was keying his young wife, yet when he spoke to me he bowed and smiled and played with his monocle. We conversed a great deal, I recall, on the subject of cheeses. During the hours of the siesta he would retire to his private apartments, while I would make love to Teresa in her pink-curtained bedroom where the pillows and sheets smelt of poppies. In this latter activity, be sure, the English milord was exceeding the duties usually expected of your *cavaliere servente*. Hand-kissing, shared coffee, attendance at operas and picnics – that, to the world, was supposed to be the extent of my relations with the Countess Guiccioli. But the Count knew there was more to it, as I say; and I knew that he knew; and he knew that I knew that he knew. Oh the infinite wisdom there can be in such profound carnal knowledge!

Then, abruptly, the Count removed my mistress to Bologna, where he possessed another little bundle of estates. It may have been humiliating, but what could I do but follow? I remember the three of us going together to the theatre to see a performance of Alfieri's tragedy *Mirra*. In this play the heroine is loved by her father, and the fruit of their incest is a beautiful child called Adonis. I could not watch the last act for my tears.

At the end of the month of August, I had Allegra fetched from Venice to keep me company in Bologna. I was amused to find that she could now speak only Italian, and that in the Venetian dialect. '*Bon di, Papa!*' she would say. She sang these sad songs to her doll, sitting under the ilex tree that grew in the garden of the palazzo where I had rented an apartment. She had not changed essentially since last I had seen her, yet she had grown much in her infant's mind, becoming more of the same. She was now a real Byron, complete with Augusta's incapacity to pronounce the letter 'r', with my pout and the family dimple in her chin, her eyebrows forever drawn into a frown, her skin as white as snow, and her voice soft. It was almost as though her mother had no part of her. And when I encountered the strength and unswervability of her temper, I had even more reason for knowing Allegra was mine.

One afternoon she came with me to the Campo Santo, where I gossiped with the gravedigger. He had peopled several cells with the skulls which his spade had turned over. I amused myself by contrasting my daughter's beautiful and innocent little face with one skull in particular, dated 1776, which once had been covered (so the gravedigger said) by the features of the most lovely woman that was ever in Bologna, noble and rich. I looked from that skull to Allegra; from Allegra to that skull. In that moment I had the most horrible presentiments, and my shivers, made the gravedigger imagine that I was suffering some kind of epileptic attack. 'No! No!' I cried. 'It is just the notion that *this* –' (and I pointed to the skull) – '*this* was once a beautiful woman!' He could not understand that it was not some general dread of mortality which consumed me, but a precise and most particular horror that human female beauty should be subject to death. It seems to me still that it is little matter what becomes of us 'bearded men', but I hate and detest the notion of a beautiful woman lasting less than a beautiful tree, than her own picture, than her own shadow, which won't change so to the sun as her face to the mirror.

That September the Count went back to Ravenna,

having given his uxorious consent to the notion that Teresa should now accompany me to Venice, where her ailments might be mended by a physician called Dr Aglietti. The autumn saw us approximating to a kind of bliss in my country house at La Mira, though my mistress's ills were certainly not to be sniffed at – she had, at this time, the piles, and a prolapsed womb. Allegra of course stayed with us, and we would no doubt have looked to any stranger like a perfect married family: Papa, his lovely young bride, and his equally lovely young daughter. This idyll survived until November, when Teresa's husband bore her back to Ravenna, and I fell sick for a week or more with a fever contracted after being drenched in a thunderstorm. Teresa-less, but still blessed with Allegra, I threw myself into *Don Juan* for relief, taking my hero and his delicious Haidee back to the sunlit shores of Greece, composing some 110 stanzas before I received a frantic letter from the Count Guiccioli at Christmas informing me that his wife had been taken desperately ill, and without my immediate presence it was feared she would die. What could I do but roll out the Napoleonic coach again?

It took until May for the husband to catch us in the act. She laughed at him. I was ashamed. The scandal became gigantic. Priests and cardinals came and went. Not batting a pretty eyelid, Teresa gave them statement after statement in which she defended her own misconduct with me by accusing the Count of sexual perversions. The cardinals wrote it all down and took it to Rome. When the Pope read it, he pronounced that a separation was in order. Teresa was to go back to her father, the Count Gamba, while Guiccioli was ordered to provide her with alimony of 1200 crowns a year. Teresa went to the country house of the Gambas. The first night I lay with her there, I asked idly about the nature of her husband's crimes in bed. He was impotent, she told me, and couldn't even come if she played with his member. His only sexual release had been achieved by throwing cream buns at her while he played with himself. I thought of the Pope and his cardinals mulling over this in the Vatican, and very nearly died of the giggles.

Don Juan began to be published in England. Murray told me it did not sell well, and sent along an article in *Blackwood's* in which my finest poetic child was described as 'filthy and impious'. Teresa's disapproval hurt me deeper, but then she has no English and it may have been the French translation.... No, I cannot permit myself such disingenuousness! She hated the Don, and there's an end of it. Perhaps there is such a thing as a male literature; I mean, a world of some books which no woman would like? To the reader who happens to be a man, I shall say only in defence of Donny Johnny what I said once to my friend Douglas Kinnaird: Confess, confess, you dog, and be candid, that it is the sublime of *that there* sort of writing. It may be bawdy, but is it not good English? It may be profligate, but is it not *life*, is it not *the thing*? Could any man have written it who has not lived in the world? And tooled in a post-chaise? In a hackney coach? In a gondola? Against a wall? In a court carriage? In a vis-a-vis? On a table? (and under it?) ... Ah, well, I had such projects for the Don, but cant is so much stronger than cunt nowadays, that the benefit of experience in a man who has well weighed the worth of both monosyllables must be lost to despairing posterity.

Teresa's brother Pietro now introduced me to an alternative to verse: namely, Italian politics. I was admitted to the secret fraternity of the Carbonari, just after my thirty-third birthday, on the midnight of which I remember I went to my bed with a heaviness of heart at having lived so long, and to so little purpose. I was bored. I was gloomy. Boredom and gloom are a part of my nature, and now, denied an escape from myself in the crazy high jinks of *Don Juan*, I sought to lift my spirits by growing absorbed in the Revolution. But the Revolution failed, as revolutions do, and I was left with a house full of arms and ammunition.

It was at this point – on Thursday, the first day of March, 1821 – that I said good-bye to Allegra. There had been soldiers shot in the street to the front of my house, and murder in the gardens at the back. I decided it was imprudent to keep my little girl in a dwelling that had been made into an arsenal. Taking Teresa's advice, I sent her to be educated at the Capucine Convent of San Giovanni, in Bagnacavallo. The school was new (founded in 1818), and the fees were high (seventy scudi per half year). The nuns were not devils nor dunces nor cruel disciplinarians. I made sure that Allegra was happy there, and I considered I'd done well by her. Claire's vitriolic letters of protest went over my head. I knew in my conscience that I'd spared neither trouble nor expense in rearing my daughter so far, and what harm could there be in my plan to have her brought up as a Roman Catholic, which I look upon as the best religion as it is assuredly the oldest of the various branches of Christianity. I am really a great admirer of tangible religion. I liked the idea of Allegra having her hands full. It is by far the most elegant worship, hardly excepting the Greek mythology. What with incense, pictures, statues, altars, shrines, relics, and the real presence, confession, absolution – there is something to grasp at. Besides, it leaves no possibility of doubt; for those who swallow their Deity, really and truly, in transubstantiation, can hardly find anything else otherwise than easy of digestion. The gist of her mother's objection was that Allegra might grow up to be like the Countess Guiccioli. I did not see that fate as so very disastrous.

If Clairmont shrieks, can Shelley be far behind? My splendid-hearted friend appeared now in Ravenna, ostensibly to give me an elegy he had written for Keats, really to spy out the convent and report back to Claire. We *did* talk of Keats, whose work as it happens I rather intensely dislike, considering it the onanism of poetry, piss-a-bed stuff by a crybaby forever frigging his own imagination. Still, on reading over Shelley's *Adonais*, I confess I was troubled. Keats had burst a blood-vessel in Rome; destroyed, Shelley said, by the world's brutal rejection of his genius. He had died young and poor, misunderstood and miserable. When Shelley had gone, I sat down and read *Endymion* again. To be blunt, I still found it just so much jam. But I made up my mind that on the subject of young poets who die young, it is better to suspend any judgement; especially if the dead poet can inspire a good poem from a spirit like Shelley. . . . I decided then never to say another word against John Keats.

More to the point, Shelley visited Allegra in her

convent. Despite his anti-clericalism, he had then to admit that the Reverend Mother and the Sisters were not engaged in damaging the child's soul, nor her mind, nor her body. Exactly what he told Claire, I have no means of knowing; but to Teresa, he said that he approved of our arrangements.

Shelley left Ravenna in the third week of August, and soon after that I elected to follow him, taking a house at Pisa called Casa Lanfranchi, where I established Teresa and her family as well as my beasts (*viz.* five peacocks, three guinea-fowl, an Egyptian crane, some monkeys, and a crow). My new dwelling, on the Lungarno, was large and magnificent, which it needed to be, in view of these dependants.

I met with three ghosts from my own past on the way to Pisa. First, on the road between Imola and Bologna, having stopped to consider the view from a crucifix, I saw another carriage toiling up the mountain in my direction, and when it drew level, and I looked through its window, I saw an old familiar face before me. 'Clare!' I cried. It was my old school friend, and that chance meeting annihilated for a moment all the years between the present time and the days of Harrow. It was a new and inexplicable feeling to me, like rising from the grave. Clare too was much agitated, more even, in appearance, than myself, for when I took his hand in mine I could feel his heart beat to the fingers' ends – unless indeed it was the pulse of my own which made me think so. We were but five minutes together, and in the public road, but I hardly recollect an hour of my whole existence which could be weighed against those minutes for intensity. We talked of nothing – of how we had changed and not changed. Then we parted, going our separate ways. A trivial encounter, and yet it still shakes me to remember it, for Clare was like a revenant from the past.

The second ghost I saw was a grave disappointment, for there, in Bologna, Samuel Rogers stepped into my coach and travelled with me until we reached Florence. After hours of his malicious conversation, I began to wonder what I had ever found to like in the man's dull verse. And it *is* dull – and silly – the product of a dessicated mind which long ago lost contact with any tiny clockwork heart there may ever have been in its vicinity. Sam Rogers is a banker, and the son of a banker. I can't think now that he was ever much of a poet. And yet it was this old calculating machine who first introduced me to Caro Lamb, as it were, by dropping *Childe Harold* slap-bang in her hot promiscuous lap.... For that, again, I have nothing to thank him for. With good luck, and some care on my part, I shan't have to see my second ghost any more.

As for the third ghost, I never saw her at all, but I know that she saw me. I had made it a condition of my removal to Pisa, that La Clairmont should not be of the party. Shelley protested at first, but I dug in my heels, so he told her to go. Somewhere on the road beyond Empoli my carriage crossed with the oncoming public coach from Pisa in which Allegra's mother was travelling to Florence. She saw me, since she wrote and told me so; I did not see her, for which I have to thank the Kindly Ones. Clare followed by Claire, with fat Rogers in between – my ghosts summed up a life gone dead on me.

For my motive in moving to Pisa was not just to establish better lodgings for the upkeep of my menagerie, nor even to chat with Shelley every day. I desired to break with the pattern my existence at Ravenna had fallen into. I wanted new people to talk to, and new things to do. With Teresa at my side, I now kept open house in a way I never quite aspired to try before. As well as the Shelleys, and the Gambas, my friends included Edward and Jane Williams, Shelley's cousin Thomas Medwin, and an Irishman called John Taaffe who was busy translating Dante without knowing much Italian (or, for that matter, English). Him I liked. In the January, our small circle was further enlarged by the arrival of a noisy sometime pirate named Edward Trelawny, six foot high, with raven-black hair which curls thickly and shortly like a Moor's, dark-grey expressive eyes, an overhanging brow and upturned lips, a kind of half-Arab Englishman. I commissioned this creature to build boats for Shelley and myself, though on second glance I didn't much like him. Still, it might yet be possible to make a gentleman out of Trelawny, if only you could persuade him to wash his hands and stop telling lies.

Our nest of singing birds did not last long. By February, Shelley fell out with me, appointing himself the advocate for Claire. The cause of our quarrel was, thus, the question of the upbringing of Allegra. In this, I believed, and still believe, that I had her best interests at heart; but I must confess that I was also irked irrelevantly by La Clairmont's *using* first our daughter, and then Shelley, to get at Teresa and myself. Every attack she made upon convents and convent-bred women seemed to me just another sly thrust at Teresa, and her onslaughts upon Catholic education in general served only to get my back up. Shelley supported Claire, for reasons of his own, possibly religious, probably amatory. I told him to mind his own poetic business.

This month began with an unexpected letter from my banker. His name is Ghigi, and he deals with the convent for me. In his letter he reported that poor Allegra was sick with a fever. I did not think too much of it. Everyone living in Venice or in the Romagna suffers from these tertians from time to time. Besides, Ghigi was quite adamant that the sickness was slight. All the same, when he wrote again, saying that Allegra had taken a turn for the worse, I sent couriers straight to Ravenna, demanding that the nuns should call in a specialist physician from Bologna if necessary. Whether this was done, I still don't know. But Ghigi wrote every day, as I instructed him. He kept me informed. And at length came this letter, just a week ago: Allegra was better. She was restored to herself again. She was as spoiled and sweet and wantonly wilful as ever, making the nuns' lives a misery, asking for Turkish delight. . . .

Then Teresa came into my study the day before yesterday. This in itself made me start, since she rarely disturbs me when I am writing. I saw from her face that something was terribly wrong.

'Byron,' she said. 'There is a letter from Ghigi.'

'Allegra,' I said. 'She is worse?'

Teresa burst into tears. Then I knew.

I am making arrangements for my child's body to be conveyed by ship to England for burial. I would like her to be buried in Harrow Church. Near the door, on the left hand side as you enter, there is a monument with a tablet containing these words:

When sorrow weeps o'er Virtue's sacred dust,
Our tears become us, and our Grief is just:
Such were the tears she shed, who grateful pays
This last sad tribute of her love and praise.

I recollect these lines (though it is many years since I saw them), not from anything remarkable in the sentiment or its expression, but because from my seat in the gallery of the church when I was a pupil at Harrow I had generally my eyes fixed on that monument. As near it as convenient I would wish Allegra to be buried, and on the wall a marble tablet placed, with these words upon it:

In memory of
ALLEGRA
daughter of Lord Byron,
who died at Bagnacavallo,
in Italy, April 20th, 1822,
aged five years and three months.
I shall go to her, but she shall not return to me.
2nd Samuel, xii, 23.

But if the churchwarden should deem it unfit to admit the body of a natural child inside the church, let him plant a rose-tree in that graveyard in her memory.

As for the rest, it is God's will. Let us mention it no more.

CHAPTER EIGHTEEN

A Second Postscript: 31st August, 1822

Once more I break the seals on my little purple parcel. My song of myself is done, but now there is another death I must record. My mother always swore death comes in threes, like the Fates and the Furies. No doubt she was right; – in which case, who is the third? From the sweat that drops down on the page where I'm writing these words, who can doubt who the third must be? And death is a country more alluring to me now than Italy, or Greece, or anywhere under the moon, since those few whom I love began to go there. No, no – no histrionics, if you don't mind, Lord Albé. You are not dying, more's the pity, or no more so than any other day. You have a touch of fever, that is all, brought on by that mad necessary swim, two weeks ago, under the sun, at noon, at Viareggio, as Shelley's body lay burning on its pyre.... Tell the story in order. Your way is to begin with the beginning.

It began, then, early this year, when I had the 'pirate' Trelawny (whom I suspect of having been nothing worse than an ordinary able seaman, but no matter), when I had our new friend Edward Trelawny build boats, one for Shelley, one for me. Mine is a yacht which I call the *Bolivar*. Shelley's was a half-decked craft, not much bigger than a ship's tender, which as a compliment patched over our past quarrels he christened the *Don Juan*. My friend's delight in this vessel was intense; like a child, as they say, with a new toy. Shelley was always inordinately fond of ships and sailing, wind and water; far more so than I. Remember the last verse of his *Adonais*:

> *The breath whose might I have invoked in song*
> *Descends on me; my spirit's bark is driven,*
> *Far from the shore, far from the trembling throng*
> *Whose sails were never to the tempest given....*

Well, one day early last month – it must have been the 11th of July, just after Leigh Hunt arrived from London with his family – I heard Trelawny shouting my name as he rode into the courtyard, on a white horse, like something out of the Apocalypse. 'What's the matter?' I called down. The matter was Shelley. Shelley was missing at sea. Trelawny had ridden all the way from Lerici to tell me so. Three days before, said Trelawny, he had stood in the bows of my *Bolivar* and watched with foreboding as Shelley and Williams weighed anchor and sailed the *Don Juan* out of the harbour at Leghorn. Their intention was to make the short voyage from Leghorn to Lerici, further along the coast, where Shelley has made his home since his quarrel with me. They should have sailed out of Leghorn at dawn, said Trelawny, but a thunderstorm came up, delaying them, and it was in fact noon when they cleared the harbour bar and stood out to sea. Trelawny, who looks after my yacht, and more or less lives on it, told me that he'd intended to accompany the *Don Juan* to Lerici, on account of the unsettled weather and my vessel being the larger and more capable. The only reason he hadn't, he said, was the port authorities. At the last minute they forced him to remain in the Leghorn harbour, some objection being raised against his clearance papers. So Trelawny had to stand there and watch the small Shelley boat sail under a lowering sky, and as he did he was suddenly filled with such a sense of doom and disaster, he told me, that he sent a crony running up to the tower on the mole to observe through a telescope the vessel's progress out to sea. When this crony came back to him, Trelawny said, he reported that about ten miles out he had seen the topsails coming down on the *Don Juan* as she pushed into a squall sweeping across the Bay of Spezia. Then the air grew dark with rain and thick mists hid the little boat from view, and when he looked again he could see nothing.

In the next twenty-four hours, Trelawny questioned every fisherman who sailed in or out of Leghorn. Not one had seen the *Don Juan*, nor a trace of her existence. So on the second day, he rode to Lerici. Shelley was not there. Mary, wild with grief, was searching the coast for a sign of him. She'd found nothing, said Trelawny. The *Don Juan* had disappeared. And Shelley was probably drowned, he said. Dead, he said.

In my heart, I agreed with Trelawny, but my mind didn't want to know. 'Isn't it possible,' I asked him, 'that they were driven out to sea?'

'It is possible,' said Trelawny.

'In which case,' I said, 'they could be safe in Corsica for all we know.'

I was clutching at straws, and we both knew it. But it was absolutely intolerable to me, in that moment, even to suppose that so vital a heart as was Shelley's was now stopped for ever. 'Go straight back to the *Bolivar*,' I instructed Trelawny. 'Keep searching until you find them.'

It took five days. On the morning of the 16th came the news that two bodies had been washed ashore some three or four miles beyond Viareggio. I rode there the following day, requesting permission to see them. I was shown some mounds in the sand between the rocks, the health authorities having ordered immediate burial in lime in accordance with stupid local regulations. I said to Trelawny: 'But if they don't let us see them, how can we be sure it's them at all?' Trelawny did not look at me as he answered: 'I saw them. Williams' body was all swollen from the sea, but just recognisable. As for Shelley – the fishes had eaten his face, and his corpse was in an advanced state of decomposition, but I know without a doubt that it was him.'

'How?' I demanded. 'How do you know it was Shelley?'

Trelawny handed me a sea-stained book.

'Because this was in his pocket,' he explained.

I took the book – what was left of it, broken and rotting – and it fell to pieces in my fingers, but not before I realised that it was a copy of Keats' *Poems* of 1820, doubled back at 'The Eve of St Agnes', as if its reader, in the act of reading, had hastily thrust it away to contend with something more urgent. In this, and remembering the calm with which Shelley had viewed the prospect of drowning when once in a storm with me, the only thing that surprises is the violence done to the Keats.

The massy earth and sphered skies are riven!
I am borne darkly, fearfully, afar;
Whilst, burning through the inmost veil of Heaven,
The soul of Adonais, like a star,
Beacons from the abode where the Eternal are.

That my friend foresaw just such an end for himself in the last stanza of his elegy for John Keats is no more than what I would have expected of him. I don't believe in sentimentalising the dead any more than the living, and I positively refuse to blaspheme against his memory by now turning pious about the purest rankest atheist I ever met. Yet here is a rare spirit gone, and a man about whom the world was ignorantly and brutally mistaken. It will do justice to him now, perhaps, when he can be no better for it. For myself, I am proud of the fact that Shelley was my friend; and grateful to him for being a good friend to me; and glad that before his death we had patched up our differences. Strange unlikely twist, but I think it was Allegra's death which brought us together again. Unlike her mother, he did not lecture me regarding my neglect of her once she was gone, but when he saw my grief and remorse and guilt in those black days Shelley was comfort itself. I say then again that here without doubt is the one poet among all my contemporaries whom I reckon my peer and my brother, and that Shelley was without exception the best and least selfish man I ever knew.

It was, of course, quite intolerable to any of those who had loved him, that Shelley's mortal remains should lie in an unmarked grave on an open beach. Negotiations were begun with the authorities for permission to disinter the two bodies and to have them reburied in the Protestant Cemetery in Rome, where Shelley's son William is buried, and indeed John Keats. Letters went back and forth on the matter for nearly a month. Then, my original request having been rejected by some petty Giacomo-in-office, I at last obtained permission to dig up poor Shelley, and Williams, and to have their two bodies cremated there on the shore. Truth to tell, it struck me that the pagan ring of this might be more in accord with what Shelley himself would have wanted, and Mary thought so too, and gave her agreement, so we made no further appeals to clerks or to priests. I arranged for Mary Shelley and Jane Williams to be escorted here to Pisa, where I put my Casa Lanfranchi at their disposal for as long as they cared to stay. Then, on the 15th of this month, I rode north in my coach with Trelawny and Hunt to Viareggio, where, the following morning, we performed our grisly task on that desolate shore.

We started with Williams. The body uncovered, it was dragged across the sand employing boathooks. Trelawny had constructed a capacious iron box, sitting on four legs, in which the bodies were to be consumed. We had some trouble fitting Williams in – not because his corpse was large, but because his flesh had deteriorated into a gummy shapeless mess, more like the remains of a sheep than a human being, and bits of it came away on the boathooks and had to be shovelled up again from where they lay scattered on the hot yellow sand. At last the ghastly hotchpotch was quite accumulated.

Trelawny lit a stick and tossed it into the box. The pyre blazed fiercely, and we assisted it along by throwing in flaming brandy-soaked rags, as well as wine and incense, the latter in an attempt to drown the foul stench which came off it. The heat was so intense that the air quivered. I stood quite close, observing how the flames changed in their colour during the burning. When the body was ash, the fire itself turned silver.

I suppose, in all honesty, that there was very little difference between the appearance of Shelley's corpse and what I'd just seen of Williams. Yet somehow it *seemed* worse, far worse, for the reason that I was possessed in gazing down upon that magma of putrid slime with a most vivid remembrance of Shelley talking, walking, waving his hands, rushing up stairs to meet me (always two steps at a time), Shelley's eyes and his lips and his seemingly unquenchable energy. Yet here it was, quenched all right, in this repulsive porridge of putrefaction. The smell was appalling. Hunt was choking on his handkerchief. I felt dizzy with disgust.

To Trelawny I said: 'I'd like to keep the skull.'

He grinned at me nastily, yet bent to oblige. However, in attempting to wrench off the skull from the spine, he broke it into pieces. I knelt and picked up fragments from the sand, but the smell was too vile in my nostrils, and splinters went into my fingertips, so I soon desisted.

I compelled myself not only to observe, but to assist in the cremation of Shelley. Trelawny lit the pyre. I poured on the wine and the incense, also some sachets of cinnamon which made the flames crackle and turn from blood-red to sea-blue. Hunt, having been sick behind a rock, was just standing there, staring.

Trelawny had stripped to the waist. Sweat streamed down his face (or it might have been tears). He spread out his arms and as the fire raged most he shouted: 'I restore to Nature through fire the elements of which this man was composed: earth, air, and water. Everything is changed but nothing is annihilated. And he is now once more a part of that which he worshipped.'

Hunt said: 'Amen.'

I clenched my fists and shook my head in fury. This was *Shelley* they were talking about, and I knew that the intelligence which was finally being consumed in that funeral pyre had been far too subtle and too various for such pantheistic formulae. It flashed through my mind to try to mutter a prayer I learned long ago, from an Armenian monk on the isle of San Lazzaro, a prayer they call the Jesus Prayer, which some of them pray without ceasing: *'Lord Jesus Christ, Son of God, have mercy on me, a sinner.'* Only, of course, for Shelley's sake, I tried to say *him* and not *me*. But the words would not come out, as I hope for no worse cause than that my throat was now parched and choked up with smoke and my tongue felt so swollen and thick in my mouth that I thought that I'd be strangled. I contented my momentary impulse towards Christianity, therefore, with a mental recitation of the beautiful prayer to the Virgin which so often I have heard from Teresa's lips, and most wish that I had heard from Allegra's: *'Holy Mary, Mother of God, pray for us sinners, now and at the hour of our death. . . .'* Then the tears came to my eyes, and would not stop.

I walked into the sea to purge my grief. Yet, more than that, I know I felt the need for absolution. I stripped off my shirt and my breeches and plunged into the waves as naked as the day that I was born. They tell me that I swam out to the *Bolivar*, where she rode at anchor perhaps a mile and a half from the shore. On the way back I was seized with a cramp, and started to vomit. Little gobbets of bile floated from me as I swam. It was late afternoon when I limped shivering from the sea again, and wrapped myself up in my cloak, and made my way back to the others. The sun still blazed down, but the funeral pyre was just smouldering. When I inspected the contents of the iron box, I saw that Shelley was now so much ash – with the exception, that is, of his *heart*, which lay there red and glowing, the only live ember, refusing to be destroyed or even divided.

Trelawny grew strangely distressed by the fact that this organ would not burn. He pierced it with a sharp stick and plucked it from the box. He held the heart up to his nose and sniffed at it, looking for all the world like a monkey suspicious of some unfamiliar food. Then he held it close to his ear, and shook it gently, as if it was a watch that might need mending. The heart was now gradually turning black, as I saw, and shrivelling; wrinkles appeared in it like the veins in a leaf that has fallen. But the heart didn't look like a leaf; it was more like a big rotten prune.

I fetched my hip-flask from the carriage and poured brandy on it. But the shrunken heart, though it bubbled, still refused to burn. In the end, Trelawny speared it again with his stick and then dipped it in the sea. The heart emerged steaming and hissing, and with blood oozing from it. I took it and dropped it in the wine jug and bore it to my carriage. (Later, I learned from a physician here in Pisa that in cases of death from drowning or other suffocation, the victim's heart is often gorged with blood, so that as a consequence it proves the more difficult to consume by fire, especially in the open air.)

Trelawny scooped up Shelley's ashes and poured them into an urn. We placed the urn in my carriage beside the wine jug. We washed our hands and our faces and rode back to the town, arriving at Viareggio just as the sun began to sink into the sea. Then the three of us went to a tavern, where we dined well. Trelawny and Hunt had lamb, while I ate a fish. I think that between us we drank seven bottles of wine. We talked about the Greeks and the Turks, and the eloquence of action, and the emptiness of words. I remember that I told them that I mean to go to Greece to be a soldier. Trelawny said that I would die there. I insisted that all three of us should drink to it.

It was past midnight when we got into my carriage. Hunt and Trelawny were drunk, but I had drunk my way through drunkenness and was now as sober as a stone. As the carriage wound down through the woods towards Pisa, my two companions soon fell asleep, but I didn't. I sat clutching the earthen wine jug with Shelley's heart in it. My cheeks were aflame with sunburn and my bones felt racked from the sea. I thought of *Don Juan* and Greece, and I thought of my mother. I thought of how my father had separated from my mother and then gone to live with his sister in France, and I wondered if my father had loved his sister as much as I had loved mine. I thought of a black French fringe and a doom top. I thought of snow. I decided I'd offer to pay the travelling expenses for Augusta and her drone of a husband, if only she'd come out to Italy and live where I could see her. I thought of Allegra in her lead-lined coffin. I made up my mind to give Shelley's heart to Mary Shelley. I thought of a thousand things, and then tried to think about nothing. The minute I tried to think about nothing, I wanted to piss. So I had the carriage stop, and got out, and pissed long and blissfully in the darkness, unbuttoning and buttoning with one hand, with all the time that earthen jug in the other. As I pissed, gazing heavenwards, I saw a star fall straight out of the night, and I watched it fall. I knew then for a certainty that the third death would be mine, and the thought did not displease me. I got back into the carriage with a shout which woke up Hunt and Trelawny. I threw back my head and howled my Albanian howl. This delighted my companions, who joined in, Hunt the alto, Trelawny a bass wolf to my tenor. We sang, we laughed, we shouted, all the long way home.

THE END OF THE MEMOIRS OF LORD BYRON

EPILOGUE

LORD BYRON DIED one year and nine months after Shelley, and two years almost to the day after Allegra, on Monday the 19th of April, 1824. He was at Missolonghi, on the north shore of the Gulf of Patras, where he had gone to fight for the Greeks in their struggle to free themselves from centuries of Turkish oppression. The cause of his death appears to have been uremia, complicated by rheumatic fever and the attentions of four doctors who favoured bleeding as the cure for everything. After an autopsy, his body was embalmed, the lungs being removed and placed in an urn which was deposited in the church at Missolonghi, but subsequently stolen. Lord Byron's other internal organs, contained in four jars, were shipped back to England with the rest of his body, and after lying in state in London and a magnificent three-day funeral procession north, these collected works were buried in the family vault at Hucknall Torkard, Nottinghamshire, near Newstead Abbey, on Friday the 16th of July.

Two months before that burial, on Monday the 17th of May, a committee consisting of John Cam Hobhouse, Thomas Moore, John Murray, and representatives of the poet's wife Lady Byron and his half-sister the Hon. Augusta Leigh, tore up every page of the only two known copies of the manuscript of his *Memoirs*, and burned the pieces in the grate of his publisher's office in Albermarle Street. Of all those present, only Moore protested, and that perhaps mostly for financial reasons (he had sold the copy entrusted to his care to Murray, and feared that he might be required to give the money back). Hobhouse, who was Byron's executor, wrote in his private journal at the time of the burning: 'The whole *Memoirs* were fit only for a brothel, and would damn Lord B. to everlasting infamy if published.'

WD06/06/01